UNKNOWN DESTINATION

UNKNOWN DESTINATION

MAYA RASKER

BALLANTINE BOOKS
NEW YORK

A Ballantine Book
Published by The Ballantine Publishing Group
Translation copyright © 2002 by The Ballantine Publishing Group,
a division of Random House, Inc.

Originally published as *Met onbekende bestemming*
by Prometheus, Amsterdam, in 2000.

Publication of this book has been made possible with the financial
support from the Foundation for the Production and Translation
of Dutch Literature.

www.ballantinebooks.com

Library of Congress Cataloging-in-Publication Data
can be obtained from the publisher upon request.

ISBN 0-345-44676-3

Manufactured in the United States of America

First American Edition: February 2002

10 9 8 7 6 5 4 3 2 1

UNKNOWN DESTINATION

PROLOGUE

IN THE REALIZATION that my language is powerless to describe what has happened in the seven years since I first met her, I am compelled to recount—no matter how inadequately—the story of my wife, the beautiful Raya Mira Salomon, who disappeared on the night of August 31, 1997, our daughter's sixth birthday, at the age of thirty-seven.

She left behind a suitcase full of papers: a photograph album, childhood postcards, letters, thoughts jotted down on scraps of paper. A year after her disappearance I opened the suitcase, in order to bury her. No trace of her had been found and I—her husband—wanted to begin the farewell, so that I could assume the new status of widower. The widower of Raya Mira Salomon.

But she was not dead, nor was she willing to keep silent. Opening her suitcase did not enable me to take leave of her, as I had hoped; again I got to know the woman I lived with for seven years: again I promised to be faithful to her until parted by death. What was intended as a liberation became a pact: more powerful than death, more intense than love, more implacable than fidelity.

With the lid of the suitcase in my hand, the widower in me died, and for the second time I married the beautiful, inscrutable Raya Mira Salomon.

1

Think

ONE

RAYA MIRA SALOMON DISAPPEARED on the evening of August 31, 1997, according to a tried-and-true formula: she went out to get a pack of cigarettes at the café around the corner and never came back.

In retrospect, I am not surprised that she disappeared as she did. She had a way of obstinately clinging to clichés: she swore by a certain washing powder because it smelled like her grandmother's house, and she hated French cars. She was uncompromising in her clichés, referring to them not as clichés, but as principles—thus ensuring her moral rectitude, even when there was no question of right or wrong, but only of personal preference.

Later on I often wondered why she didn't choose a more tasteful farewell scenario: stealing away after a long stroll along the beach perhaps, or disappearing without a trace after a lonely mountain climb—at any rate, something less banal than going out for a pack of cigarettes. Or perhaps her disappearance was as trivial in her eyes as the purchase of a box of washing powder, something so inconsequential that you do it unthinkingly.

The barman remembered seeing her. She'd asked for a pack of cigarettes and then had a whisky at the bar. Business was slow. It was raining hard, and seeing that the café depended on passersby rather than regulars, there were few customers. The man recalled that she'd refreshed her lipstick before going back outside, but he hadn't noticed anything unusual.

Nor did I have any notion that day of what was to come. As always, we celebrated the birth of our daughter with a bottle of wine from the year she was born, 1991. It was an excellent year, especially for the Riojas, which improve with each passing year. I had opened a Clos Abadia Raimat, which, although relatively young, needs a lot of oxygen to reach its peak. In the afternoon we uncorked the bottle and then each had a whisky to loosen our tongues. Raya Mira was taciturn by nature. She even continued to drink during her pregnancy, saying she wasn't planning to go through the entire nine months without opening her mouth. So it wasn't unusual for us to start with a glass of whisky. We were sitting on the deck in the shelter of an overhanging balcony, and it was raining as it rains only on a hot day in late summer. In between our glasses stood the wine bottle, soaking up the ozone. We gazed in silence at the rhododendron cuttings, which seemed to give way under the onslaught of the rain, and at the water streaming out of the leaking drainpipe, making a hole in the ground.

Raya poured herself a second glass of whisky. That wasn't unusual either. She was very self-controlled in her intemperance: sometimes one, sometimes two glasses too many, never on the verge of drunkenness and seldom with a view to communicating anything very important.

"The rhododendron is drowning," she said when the rain had stopped. In the silence which followed the downpour, we listened to the tapping of the raindrops falling from the drainpipe and looked at the fragile plants, which were almost submerged.

THE GARDEN wasn't my idea. I don't like gardening. Nor could Raya be accused of any particular interest in the care and maintenance of plants. When I brought her flowers, she'd toss them into the wastebasket as soon as they began to wilt; it never occurred to her to change the water or trim the stems. And yet she was the one who suddenly moved heaven and earth to get hold of this tiny patch of garden, even though it meant giving up a substantial amount of space: Raya's house in the dunes and my upstairs flat in town. But it wasn't about the garden, as I later realized; it wasn't even about the child that she was secretly carrying. We hadn't been in the new house for more than a day and a night when I found Raya sitting on the deck in the chill of an autumn morning, with her hands cupped around a mug of coffee and her gaze fixed on infinity.

Later she dutifully planted the rhododendron her mother had given her, and every year she obsessively took cuttings from the plant, knowing how high the mortality rate was in her hands. At the end of the summer she said, "The rhododendron is drowning," and in the winter, "The rhododendron is freezing," and in the summer, "The rhododendron is drying out." And from one season to the next she sat on the deck every morning at quarter past six, staring beyond the rhododendrons into nothingness.

WHERE DO YOU DISAPPEAR to when you're as beautiful as Raya Mira Salomon was on that evening in August? With painted lips, as always, but now with red polish on her nails and her hair gathered up with a single hairclip. Although the weather was oppressively hot, she was wearing leather trousers, her feet bare—a minor concession—her toenails painted, as if she were trying to add a little decorum to her feet. Raya esteemed her body; there was little that betrayed that she had borne a child. A small, elegant underbelly that could no longer be denied was carried as a badge of motherhood, like the crow's-feet around her eyes and a few dozen gray hairs.

It was a while before I could recall what else she was wearing that evening. I had to examine the contents of her closet to see which items of clothing were missing. It hadn't bothered me, this gap in my memory, but the detectives considered the information necessary for an accurate "missing person" description. Something else I didn't see as important at the time. She must have been wearing the silk jacket I gave her one Christmas, and the bustier she picked up at the local Hema store.

Raya liked to shop at Hema. It was like her grandmother's washing powder: a conviction that refused to die.

I FILLED THE WINEGLASSES and went into the kitchen to slice some bread. The tapping coming from the drainpipe accelerated to a soft rattle.

"I'm going to get some cigarettes," she said, and slipped into the sandals that were standing near the kitchen door.

That is the last image I have of her: ten red toenails in open shoes on the doormat next to the kitchen door.

"It's starting to rain again!" I called out, but she was already gone.

WHERE DO YOU GO with painted toenails in open shoes and leather trousers that weren't made for walking in the rain? The café is just around the corner, and maybe she ran to beat the rain, but she was wet when she walked into the café. The barman gave her a towel to dry her face; he remembered that there was a trace of lipstick on it.

In the weeks following her disappearance those feet kept reappearing in my dreams. Coquettish toenails that sprouted like flowers from the earth where the murderer had buried her. Flecks of red on the duckweed covering the lake she'd walked into. Severed toes, red against the gray of the gravel along the railway track.

Later they appeared during the day as well: her toenails lay among the raspberries at the market, or sprouted from the tulips at the flower stall, or took the place of the pimiento in the olives.

I REMEMBER that the wine was exceptional. I had waited for her, so we could raise our glasses together. It was a moment we'd always cherished: the breaking of the bread, the drinking of the wine, perpetuating a pact in honor of our daughter's birthday.

I waited until the rain stopped. Raya Mira had now been gone for over an hour. Was there dread, surprise, fear? A quiet desperation came when it dawned on me that I had to do something, that it was unusual that she, my wife, had suddenly disappeared. But just as the anesthetic slowly wears off after a dental treatment, gradually giving way to the latent pain, I felt the numbness rising: from my feet, my knees, my back, along my elbows to my neck—an anesthetic that dulled the pain that was yet to come.

There was nothing I could do but lift the glass and drink the wine. (The first time my daughter sucked at my nose—she must have been quite tiny, and must have thought it was the nipple, with her lips clamped tightly around the tip of my nose and her cheeks pumping furiously in hopeful expectation of the milk that would come streaming out—it was pure poetry, a joy that exceeded the sensual.)

The sip I took that evening was like my daughter's mouth on the tip of my nose. It was the most delicious wine I have ever tasted.

At daybreak there was a ring at the door. I didn't sleep that night, although I was no longer conscious. I must have stood watch like a dog guarding its master's property, body at rest, ears pricked. The doorbell didn't startle me; my whole being was prepared for that one moment. Had she forgotten her keys? She hadn't taken her key ring, I knew that. Her vanity prevents her from using the pockets of the leather trousers. So she'll ring the bell. It's five o'clock in the morning, and she'll say, "I'm going to bed, see you later"—there are few things she considers so urgent that they have to be discussed immediately.

Had she taken revenge for that one time I'd slipped up? Had she found her Prince Charming? I would open the door with a neutral expression on my face, undress her and put her to bed, and then stand under the shower with a sense of satisfaction after this bizarre night. And later I would say, "So what was it like, the first time?"—taking pride in my self-control, pleased to be allowed to humiliate her, just for a moment.

THE ANESTHESIA of the night drained out of my body. My head thawed first; the tapping of the drainpipe was still reverberating under my skull. My fingers and toes tingled from the cold; the eye, until then focused inward, saw the sun rise, saw the little rhododendron that had survived the deluge of the previous night.

It was five o'clock in the morning and there was someone at the door. Before me stood the barman at the café where Raya went to buy cigarettes, holding her sandals in his hand. They dangled nonchalantly from a couple of fingers and only then did it dawn on me: they're empty. Raya's sandals, the ones she was wearing when she left last night. Without toenails, without feet, without wife.

The barman looked at me questioningly. I took the sandals, thanked the man, and closed the door. It didn't occur to me to ask him the questions that a person would want to ask. What are you doing here at five o'clock in the morning? When did she leave your café? And how—with whom?

I knew: she's dead.

THE BARMAN called the police. Which is peculiar, since he personally wasn't missing anyone; there was no reason for him to assume that any of the circumstances which presented themselves here called for police intervention. Nevertheless, as he stated in his deposition, he was so alarmed by the look in my eyes that he decided to inform the police that one of his customers, Mrs. Raya Mira Salomon (whom he knew) entered his place of business on the evening of August 31 around eight o'clock, and that shortly afterward, after having a whisky, visiting the ladies' room, and putting on lipstick, she left the establishment, destination unknown. While cleaning the café early that morning he had found a pair of women's sandals that he believed belonged to Mrs. Salomon, and decided to return them immediately.

He could not remember whether she was wearing other shoes when she left the café.

He had had an uneasy premonition, which was reinforced by the glazed expression on the face of Mr. Gideon Salomon when his wife's sandals were returned to him. That was when he called the officer on duty.

TWO

THE FIRST FEW WEEKS after her disappearance, nothing changed. It wasn't the first time that she'd stayed away for a while, and my days followed one upon the other much as they had always done. Not long before, I had started on a new project, another reason why all sense of time and circumstance began to desert me.

When I'm working, I see things differently. The boundary between day and night becomes blurred; the answering machine takes care of my social obligations, eating and sleeping are like going to the toilet: you yield to an urge when it makes itself felt, and otherwise you give it no thought.

I live as if I'm in an aquarium, separated from the world by water and glass. Sometimes I see a familiar face heading in my direction; it presses its nose against the glass wall that separates us, to see if everything's all right in here.

I smile and dive to the bottom.

SUMMER TURNS TO AUTUMN; it doesn't register with me. I'm working on a series of photographic interpretations of poems; there's a lot riding on this, since the idea hasn't been sold yet. Rainer Maria Rilke. Anna Akhmatova. Federico García Lorca. Salvatore Quasimodo:

Hands clasped under my head
I remembered the times I returned
to the smell of fruit drying on hurdles,
and wallflowers, lavender, ginger;
when I thought of reading softly to you
(you and I, mother in an angle of shade)
the tale of the Prodigal Son
that always followed me through the silences.

I sit down at my drawing table and leaf through the sketch-book. Drawings of a little boy—*remembered the times I returned*—remember, is that in color or black and white? The boy is sitting with his back against the planking of a shed, and next to him on the bench is an open book—*smell of fruit drying on hurdles.* What is he reading? What does he remind me of? A Brancusi, a Rodin? Sketches of a grown man, hands folded under his head. In an angle of shade *(you and I, mother).*

But for the dead there is no return
and no time, not even for a mother
when the road calls.

I am standing on a mountain path and it's indescribably hot. The landscape lies at my feet, as if dead. Even the crickets are silent, and the lizards have taken shelter under damp stones. The hills to the left and right of the path slope gently, like the sheet under which Raya Mira is lying asleep. Only her breathing is missing; all I hear is the panting in my own chest. The path ends at a small cemetery, a mile or so outside the village. The graveyard is walled, the wall not whitewashed but left in its original colors: brown, reddish, camouflage. From my position at the top of the path, the walls take on the contours of an open book. I look down on the right side and the left side of the book, divided in the middle by low shrubbery. The rows of graves are the lines on the page.

The tripod is screwed to the ground. I am careful to keep the camera and the rolls of film in the thermos bag, providing some protection against the heat. I take wine out of my rucksack, then bread and water, and wait until the sun goes down and the light becomes bearable.

> And no time, not even for a mother
> when the road calls.

The first hint of shadow appears; the sun surrenders. A boy appears on the road; he greets me and walks on. I take the camera, screw it onto the tripod, and follow him in the viewfinder. He reaches the cemetery and stops at one of the graves in the wall. Who is he visiting? A sister, a mother? I push the button, knowing I haven't got it yet: what matters now is the sensation, the slight pressure in the fingertips, the soft, mechanical click of the device. I push the button again, and again, as the boy leaves the cemetery. Then he sits down in the shadow of the wall—no, he's lying down, his rucksack next to him, with his hands folded underneath his head.

> In an angle of shade, you and I, mother . . .

I PUSH the button again, and then pack up my things.

"GOOD?"
"Good."
Raya is sitting on the terrace of our guesthouse: a table and two chairs on what we would call the sidewalk, but which here takes up most of the street. It's quiet in the village. The men have left for the beaches to do seasonal work; the women have withdrawn inside their houses. It's hot. On the table stands a bottle of lukewarm wine. She looks upset.
"My pen is leaking."

I see a few smudged scrawls in her notebook. Her fingers are blue. In the room her inkpot is standing in a bowl of water to keep it cool. It's no use; even the tap water is lukewarm.

"What are you writing?" Out of the corner of my eye I look to see where the landlady is.

She shrugs: "*The evening is penitent, still dreaming about noon.*"

"The evening should know better." I wipe the perspiration from my nose.

She looks at me (I wonder what she's writing?). The poems were her idea.

"The evening is cooler," I say, "more beautiful, more virginal."

"More virginal?"

"More innocent, maybe."

I go inside to get a glass. In our room I pick up the sketches I did before we left on this assignment. Portraits of a small boy, a grown man. I draw well, with charcoal, but one glance again brings home to me the pointlessness of this preliminary exercise.

"It just doesn't work, thinking ahead," I say when I'm sitting next to her again, "and I don't know how else to do it."

Raya leafs through the sketchbook.

"You have to start somewhere. It doesn't lead anywhere, but it limbers up your brain cells."

(Her papers are lying all over our house. Notebooks, scraps of paper, cuttings on all sorts of subjects. You have to start somewhere. It's like a tangle of loose threads in which no one can discern a pattern. Except for her. When she starts writing, she knows exactly which anecdote she jotted down on which pad, which quotation she underlined in which newspaper article. Settling herself at her loom, she weaves all those rags into a tapestry.)

She examines my sketches closely.

"This one is good."

"It's not a photo."

"The *drawing* is good."

THAT WAS THEN.

I stare at the drawing for a long time: the sketch of a young woman's face, resting on both hands. The face of the mother as she must have appeared in the memories of Quasimodo: dark eyes, a soft line around the lips, wrinkles of reconciliation. Isn't this what all mothers look like in the recollection of their adult children?

The hands are what she has become: an old, spent life.

Again I hear the certitude in Raya's voice: "The *drawing* is good."

I mustn't listen; I'm not a draftsman.

I sit down at the table for the next series of sketches. You have to start somewhere. It limbers up your brain cells. Akhmatova, St. Petersburg. It keeps you busy. It doesn't lead anywhere, but it keeps you limber.

> *And if a difficult path lies ahead for me,*
> *Here's an easy task for me—*

It doesn't lead anywhere. It limbers up your suffering. It suffocates your limbs.

THE COLD CREEPS up along my back. I recognize this feeling. It tingles in my feet and fingers, my back grows numb.

Why is it so cold? I draw the Neva, an ink-black circle in the ice.

Children's hands in mittens feed the ducks in the ice hole. The Neva, I have to get to St. Petersburg, I have to get there before the river freezes over and the ice hole disappears. It's October; there's still time. When does winter begin in Russia? When does a Russian winter begin?

I GET UP FROM THE DRAWING TABLE, walk into the living room, and pick up the telephone. I dial the KLM number, which I know by heart. Press 0 for last-minute travel, press 1 if you want to speak to an assistant, press 2 if you are paying by credit card. I press the keys and await the monotonous tune that puts you on hold. The phone is ringing. Someone answers.

"St. Petersburg, please. What have you got for St. Petersburg?" There is silence at the other end of the line.

"Hello! Salomon here. I want a last-minute to St. Petersburg. What have you got for me?"

I'm getting impatient. Another dimwit; you can always tell by the voice. "I'm sorry, sir," she'll say sheepishly, "it's my first day on the job. One moment, please." And then she'll try to transfer the call and disconnect me instead.

And it does remain quiet for a very long time.

"Gideon?"

I am about to ask indignantly how she knows my first name. But it's a male voice. Which is strange: the KLM doesn't use male voices on the reservations line.

"Gideon!"

Jelle again. Now how does he know it's me?

"Gideon, you called me. What's all this crap about St. Petersburg?"

"I'm not calling you; I'm calling KLM. I need to get to St. Petersburg for the Akhmatova series. Why are you calling me?"

"I'm not calling you. You're calling me. What's all this crap?"

I hang up.

Jelle. He's a loyal friend, no doubt about it, but sometimes loyal friends can be pretty irritating. The day after Raya disappeared, he came to the front door with a sleeping bag over his arm and a bottle of whisky in his hand. I accepted the whisky—it was nice of him—but I didn't need company. He called me every day until he finally realized that I was simply working. Nothing wrong. A lot to do. Ambitious plans for my poets series.

In the end he stopped leaving messages on my answering machine. That's the nice thing about loyal friends: they know when to stop.

JELLE AND I have been friends for years; he was there the night I met Raya. It was at a party given by Christian Winkler, a mutual friend—actually, we never see him anymore. Christian and a couple of friends lived in a ramshackle villa called Little Heaven on the edge of town. It was a real Pippi Longstocking house: Art Nouveau leaded glass and paneling all over this huge hall where the party was held. There would be a lot of people there I didn't know, and Jelle had to persuade me to go along. Christian did something in advertising, and I'm not too keen on parties like that. Jelle knew everybody. He knew Raya Mira too. She was on the editorial staff of some magazine he did the odd assignment for. He thought she was a bitch, a cold and self-important bitch.

I stood pressed against the wall with a whisky in my hand and, for the occasion, smoking a cigarette I'd just been given by a blond girl. This did not lead to any further exchanges. Her name was Petra and she worked as an intermediary with a temp agency. I didn't know how to follow that.

Raya Mira was sitting on the stairs on the opposite side of the hall, her eyes fixed on me. Her hands were small and old, much older than she was. She had long red nails and was wearing a dark purple velvet dress with a short skirt. Underneath, long legs in panty hose. And climbing boots. Pretty clunky, I thought.

She continued to look at me. I stared back, uninhibited by any sense of propriety. After all, she started it. Short black hair, slightly wavy. Brown eyes. Or dark green? She wasn't smoking; I noticed that. She looked like the type of girl you'd expect to smoke, the kind who suffered from some repressed neurosis, the kind who might go all hysterical at the breakfast table. I knew the type. But her hands were just lying quietly in her lap as she looked at me.

That's where my gaze finally came to rest: on old, remorseless hands against dark purple velvet. Hands made to strangle and to stroke.

"D o y o u want to sleep with me?"

We were sitting at the top of the stairs, leaning against the ban-
isters and watching the people in the hall below. They were dancing; I don't like to dance and the music was loud. I nodded.
Without a word we went downstairs and made our way to the
door. In passing I pulled Jelle toward me. He was on the dance
floor. I was fairly sure that Jelle didn't like to dance.

"I'm leaving with Raya Mira."

"Oh?"

He was holding on to the flap of my jacket. He was drunk; I
could tell by his eyes.

"Call you tomorrow," I parried, and freed myself from his grasp.

She'd come by bike, a black men's bike, a Burco. She lived on
the outskirts of town, in the dunes. I'd walked to the party. I was
of two minds: Is it trendy to let a girl do the biking, or do I offer to
pedal and let her sit on the baggage carrier? It didn't look too
sturdy. Raya Mira unlocked the bike and gave me the handlebars.
She took her place on the crossbar.

"Take Wenckebach on out; it's not as far as you think."

Her hair smelled like smoke and sea and hair spray. It was cold,
treacherously cold after the sweltering atmosphere of the party. I
thought about long legs in panty hose: Do panty hose retain heat?
I wondered if she was wearing briefs. I imagined her fluid drop-
ping slowly onto her panty shield. Warm cobwebs nestling in pu-
bic hair, like a spider's web in the morning dew. Cycling with an
erection is uncomfortable. I thought about Petra, the blond intermediary. That had a calming effect.

S h e t u r n e d o n the light in the hall.

"The bedroom's in there," she said, as if she were talking to a
dog she'd just brought home from the shelter. There's your basket.

The bedroom was small and cold. It smelled of the sea. The bed
was half-made, the duvet cover faded and outmoded. Probably a

present from her mother, I thought, when she set up house on her own. Washed-out flowers in pink and blue. The bedclothes were clammy and smelled like sleep. I went over to the window to close the curtains. The window was open—no wonder it was so cold. I tried to lift the hook so I could close the window, but it wouldn't budge. Stuck. I pulled hard and the wooden frame creaked where the hook was attached.

"What are you doing?"

Raya stood in the door of the bedroom.

"I'm closing the window."

"I always sleep with the window open."

Into your basket, doggy.

She was carrying two glasses of whisky and a cigarette. (So I was right.) She drew the curtain and sat down next to me on the bed, still wearing her hiking boots. We leaned back against the bunched-up pink-and-blue duvet. It was cold, but comfortable now.

THE STOVE IS ON. Jelle is sitting across from me; he needs a haircut; his sandy curls are tangled. He looks worried. I feel a blanket around my shoulders. It's cold, but comfortable now. He hands me a glass of whisky. We take a sip.

(She stretches her long neck. Her hands glide over my hair, my unshaven cheeks. She's kicked off her boots and she's rubbing my ankle with her foot. Like a swan. Strong, slender arms. A blow from her wing could break your arm. Especially if it's a mother with young. Her neck arches in my neck. I want to kiss, but she turns her head away. Feeling, groping, stroking, searching. Her hands guide her. Like a blind, white swan.)

"You're delirious, Gideon."

Good old Jelle. He hasn't left my side. He sits there and turns up the stove.

"The rhododendron is drowning," I say.

"I think I'll go clean up the kitchen," he says, and walks out of the room.

THREE

THE BARMAN HAD set in motion a chain of events of which I was unaware. Looking back, I was glad he'd reported the disappearance of Raya Mira. It didn't even occur to me. Detectives questioned my family; they asked friends about our marriage, about her alleged alcoholism, about the financial position in which Raya and I found ourselves. Yes, we each had life insurance in the other's name, not uncommon after the birth of a child, or so I've heard. But in this case, reason enough to carry out an in-depth investigation. After talking with my family and Jelle, they decided to leave me to myself for a while, although they did inform our family doctor.

You sometimes hear stories about people being greeted with polite sniggers when they report a disappearance. "Yes, I see. Your wife's left home. Last night? And it's now ten o'clock in the morning. Went out for a pack of cigarettes, you said? Well, sir, if I were you, I'd wait a little longer. Did she enjoy her job? New colleague at work maybe? Know what I'd suggest? You just go home, and ten to one there'll be a message on your answering machine."

Due to the gravity with which the barman apparently told his story down at the station, I was spared all that. Raya Mira Salomon's name was on the Interpol telex long before I—her husband—fully realized that she had disappeared.

FOR ME, she wasn't missing and she hadn't disappeared. She was gone, I understood that, but the implications of that fact did not even begin to sink in. The lethargy that came over me that night has never gone away. I didn't tell anyone that she had disappeared. I went to bed, slept for twenty-four hours, and then got down to work.

As if she had never left. As if she had never been there.

There were moments of pain: a brief, piercing pain that seemed to tear my body apart, the kind of pain you imagine must announce the onset of a heart attack. Raya once tried to explain to me what it was like to bear a child: the pain that rises from your belly, slices through your bone marrow, mangles your pelvis, breaks your legs. That's more or less what I felt: my intestines contracted, the air left my lungs, I retched with my entire body. Often it came quite suddenly. A moment before, I had seen her in the empty house: a shadow of Raya sitting at the table, in her chair under the reading lamp, out on the deck with a cup of coffee. It was perfidious, since not every sighting caused me to double up. I had no trouble putting away the clothes that were still lying on our bed. Without a qualm I shoved her papers to one side to make room on the table. No, it wasn't that. It was the sound of her voice, suddenly rising out of nowhere, making me moan like a woman in labor.

She talked to me, or rather, she read me the scribbles she used to leave behind for me all over the house: *You're like a thrashing chicken. For a man, the inexorability of parenthood is a matter of choice—and that's what makes it so implacable. You thrash about, but you know that soon your neck is going to be mercilessly wrung.*

(SHE ENJOYED SEEING ME wrestle with my new role as a father. She enjoyed it, but she didn't gloat. Deadly earnest, she watched me thrashing about, analyzed the restlessness that came over me when the child started to cry or I ran out of diapers

after the stores had closed, or the time I thought the girl had broken her neck when she fell out of bed. She watched in silence, and
in the evening I'd see her writing in one of her notebooks, with the
ever-present fountain pen and the eternal glass of wine. The next
morning her thoughts would be lying on the kitchen counter next
to the gas range.)

As long as I was in the darkroom, I was
safe. It had always been that way. Her voice couldn't reach me
there. She had never taken any great interest in my work, at least
not in the craft underlying the photos. The darkroom was my domain, the sanctuary of my own thoughts, and she would never in-
vade it. But as soon as I left that bastion, the spirit of Raya was
lying in wait for me. "Gideon, why don't mothers feel an aversion
to their offspring more often?"

I put my hands over my ears and hurried off to the kitchen to
make a sandwich. The counter looked like a battlefield; I couldn't
find the bread (or had I finished it?), and with half a box of corn-
flakes in my hand, I raced back to the darkroom. At the door her
voice stopped me again: "Gideon, which is a bigger lie, writing or
taking photographs?"

She looks up from the chair where she's reading. The thought
crosses my mind that she would look good in reading glasses. Some
women do.

What is a lie? Why now? Why won't you leave me alone?

After a while I didn't leave the darkroom at all except
to go to the toilet, and even that was seldom necessary. The food
was almost gone, but I wasn't hungry, and the idea of leaving the
house to go shopping filled me with an infinite dread. I knew that
Raya would be standing there, next to the salad dressings or the
cold cuts, ready to pounce on me. The last week I barely slept. The
whisky was gone, and I dreaded the moment when I would have to

go to bed without the security of drunkenness. I wouldn't survive. Like a soldier in the trenches, I holed up in the darkroom with what I needed, drifted off from time to time, slept propped against the wall or bent over the drawing table, and then went back to what I was doing.

Until I had to go to St. Petersburg. It was Akhmatova's poem that penetrated my madness:

> *And children were shoving their mittens*
> *Through the bridge's rusty iron railings*
> *To feed the greedy, gaudy ducks*
> *That somersaulted into ink-dark circles in the ice.*
> *And I thought: it's not possible*
> *That I will ever forget this.*

I was so terribly afraid that the ink-black circles in the Neva would freeze over.

"P s y c h o t i c " was the doctor's verdict. Not unusual for someone who's had a severe emotional shock. You withdraw into your own world, banish all emotion, and survive by slipping into brief delusions. And I had delusions, even though I thought they were memories or visions of fantastic assignments in the offing.

Jelle was alarmed by my phone call. For weeks he had driven by my house every morning to check whether the curtains were open. He had even looked through the mailbox, he confessed later, to make sure that I had picked up the mail. He was really worried when he saw that the kitchen was getting filthier by the day. It's at the end of the corridor, directly opposite the front door and the slit in the mailbox. In a way, he was glad I called, because it gave him an alibi to let himself into the house, using the key he'd quietly picked up from the mantelpiece.

He sat me down next to the stove and wrapped me in a blanket. Then he handed me a glass of whisky.

"You're delirious, Gideon," he said.

"The rhododendron's drowning," I answered anxiously.

He went to the kitchen and called the doctor. He didn't want to upset me, but I could see the fear in his eyes. That's one of the strange things about a psychosis: there are often moments of extreme lucidity. Except that I was convinced that he was worried about the rhododendron.

THE DOCTOR GAVE ME AN INJECTION, and after that I slept for forty-eight hours a delirious sleep in which the red toenails, which were to pursue me for so long, made their first appearance. Jelle installed himself in the side room that had long since become a repository for junk. He cleaned up the kitchen and did the shopping. He added some soil around the rhododendron and put in stakes. He stayed with me, especially since the doctor couldn't say for sure which way my psychosis would go.

When I woke up, he was sitting at the kitchen table, bent over the newspaper. There was a pan of soup on the stove. He looked up and saw in my eyes that the madness had gone.

It was time for the grief.

FOUR

I'm just a regular guy. I felt proud that the beautiful Raya Mira had thawed in my arms—and why? I didn't force myself on her; I just waited to see how her waves would hit my coast: rippling, battering, tumbling, rumbling. Sand can't break (a comforting thought); it just changes shape. You think it's the sea that's doing it, but in the end it's the grains themselves that are regrouping, returning to what they originally were. The onrushing waves are no more than a moment in the eternal monotony of taking shape, disintegrating, and regrouping. In the end, the coastline remains more or less the same.

The first night I slept with her, I was struck by the gracefulness with which she explored my body before giving herself over to me. There was no trace of the diffidence that makes girls so attractive because it appeals to your virility to take the initiative, to take them. She set the tone, dancing her solo in the icy cold of her bedroom-on-the-beach. I was no more than a bit player, following her movements like a shadow. The passionate sex you might expect—on the first night and with enough liquor in you—was not forthcoming.

It was not a disappointment, but it was a surprise, and I thought for a long time about whether I should bring it up. Maybe something like, "What do you think about when we make love?"

The thought of having to say anything at all made me uncertain. I also didn't want to know.

I HAD KNOWN WOMEN before Raya crossed my path. I'd lived with a woman and made plans. With Nanda, who worked in advertising, and with Margot, an artist I even wanted to have a child with. But there always came a moment when I thought, It's time to get out of here. With Nanda that feeling came the day we went to look at the site of a new housing estate: front garden, back garden, and four different front doors to choose from. We were standing in the middle of a sandy plain, looking at a billboard projection of the marvel that would one day arise on this unlikely spot. Smooth marketing guys representing the developer were delivering their spiel about "Cinema Park" (Nanda had set her heart on a model planned for Zarah Leander Avenue); girls from the temp agency were handing out tea in plastic cups, and the pointers swished from right to left over our heads. "Here you see the future site of the shopping center, complete with Albert Heijn supermarket and a branch of the public library. And this (with an expansive gesture in the direction of no-man's-land), ladies and gentlemen, is the harbor where a flotilla of sailboats will be moored on summer afternoons!"

It was a pathetic spectacle, a little group of people standing in the middle of a windy polder landscape, shivering with cold and clutching folders extolling the virtues of something that did not yet exist and would never come to anything. My misery was complete when I looked at the rapturous face of my fiancée. Not long afterward I broke off the relationship. She didn't understand why, which steeled me in my decision.

I'M A REAL FAMILY MAN, despite the wild oats I've sown. All I was doing was looking for my one true love. I've never wanted anything but that one true love. I have no desire to end up as a forty-three-year-old part-time father with visiting privileges, a younger girlfriend, and a flat in a nice suburb. I lean toward a soft-boiled egg for breakfast, three kids in their parents' bed before the alarm goes off, a dining set from IKEA, and going shopping on Saturday morning.

Basically I'm just a regular guy.

MY MOTHER ALWAYS SIGHED: "Ah, my boy, back again!" after which she cheerfully took delivery of the laundry bag, and sent my father upstairs with the luggage, to the room my brothers and I shared as boys. She was delighted that I had come home to the nest, after yet another failed attempt to commit my-self to a woman. With a devotion that was almost sensuous, she'd spend the evening listening to my stories: about how things hadn't worked out as I'd hoped, the shortcomings of the girl in question, and my own failings as a man. How I had longed for the feeling that this was "for always," and was filled with apprehension at the thought of the next day, and the prospect of waking up next to Nanda or Margot or Ditte or Tries for the rest of my life.

I am everything for my mother. The family is everything for her, and of all the members of our family, I am number one. I'm the youngest of three boys, and I was conceived after my father had been diagnosed with terminal cancer. The two older boys were already in primary school. In the hospital my mother mounted my father—having gotten around the nursing staff in the ICU, the drips, the respirator, and the catheter—and made herself one last child. After that he would die, and she would be carrying the son who would always be The Son.

But my father didn't die, and she's never forgiven him. Not that she wasn't fond of him. But by remaining alive he had robbed her of the valor of her deed in the ICU and the heroism of her future life as a young widow with three growing sons. After that she was never anything but your average housewife, hardworking, dedi-cated, and self-effacing.

I've often wondered whether the terminal nature of his illness wasn't a figment of her imagination, rather than the diagnosis made by my father's physicians. I don't believe in miracles. But even if it is true, even if I was born out of her interpretation of the truth, I still can't blame her.

We all spend a lot of time lying to each other.

WHENEVER I BROKE UP with a girl and made a beeline for my parents' house, I always saw to it that my laundry bag was full, my shirts unironed, and the buttons on my collar hanging at half-mast. "Oh, my poor boy," my mother would say, appalled, and she'd stay up until all hours of the night bent over her sewing basket or ironing board, righting all these wrongs.

I did my best to appear emaciated or at least unshaven and hollow-cheeked whenever I honored them with a visit and allowed her to put before me the special meatballs she'd started preparing as soon as she got my phone call. She couldn't bear the thought that one day I might walk in the door with a radiant air of "Mom, everything's absolutely perfect!" It would have been the death of her, and we both knew it.

While I was living with Nanda I did a good deal of lying too, even though they weren't lies. I was twenty-five and I wanted a house of my own with a front door and a back door and a hobby room that could later be converted into a nursery. I wanted to get away from my mother and her sewing box, away from the evasive look in my father's eyes that spoke of a failed life. I wanted to grow up, and to do so I needed Nanda and her four different front doors to choose from.

And I wasn't lying when I said I wanted to have a child with the trendy Margot, and do a photo series of her and our child and our little family, the launch of my brilliant career as a photographer. None of that was a lie; it was as true as true can be. But was it honest?

I was afraid I would never be able to break away from my mother's

Miele washing machine, and longed for a lunch box packed by my
wife's hands, filled year after year with a cheese sandwich on whole-
wheat bread, a ham sandwich on white bread, an apple, and a car-
ton of milk.

What I feared was what I most desired.

THE FIRST FEW MONTHS of love are so all-consuming.
What is that obsession to get to know each other, to explore and
to possess the other as fast as possible? It leaves no room for
thought; the endorphins rage through your body; it's all talking
and screwing and screwing and talking, as if death were on your
heels.

That was love as I knew it. But that hadn't gotten me anywhere.

The searing passion that is characteristic of the first few months
of being in love is meant only to ascertain whether you're on the
track of true happiness. As efficiently and sexily as possible, you
tick off the criteria which determine whether it's go or no go. On
the surface it's delirious love, while underneath a highly calculated
process is taking place. The ritual of courtship is nothing but the
baring of old layers of the soul, where nose and ears and eyes have
hidden their memories. Where familiarity, fears, and dreams are
concealed.

The deepest longing for security searches for a handhold, and
that search usually takes place in the kitchen. The nose hunts for
meatballs, the eyes scour the labels on cans and jars, the fingertips
run along the greasy edges of kitchen cabinets. While the body is
engaged in passionate sex, there is an autonomous compartment in
the brain where all this information is stored and compared. Compared with what you expect from life. Compared with what life
has given you.

The brain fills up with pluses and minuses, independent of the
body, which is still wandering about among all those hairs and
juices and smells, and then it goes *bleep*: it has determined whether

there is synchronism between dream and reality, or whether hope is all that remains.

Even after the bleep, not everything has been decided. It may take months before you accept the mathematical impossibility of the union you form with Nanda or Margot or Ditte or Tries. But in the first few weeks, often in the very first hour, it has all been settled. It is then only a matter of waiting for the moment of receptiveness.

WITH RAYA MIRA, everything was different. She sat on the porch of her house in the dunes on the morning after our first night, with a bathrobe over her shoulders and a cup of coffee in her hand. I awoke from an unusually deep sleep but did not experience the tingle you expect after a first night. It was not familiar, lying there alone. But neither was there the alienation you sometimes feel after spending the night with a pickup whose name was either Julia or Juliette, you can't quite remember.

I was lying in bed and she was sitting outside and that was that: a given, devoid of the hope or passion or doubt which usually accompanies the beginnings of love.

Looking back, I often asked myself what it was that kept me from being engulfed by that same unrest. And I came to this conclusion: there was nothing to be found in the depths of my memory that provided any guidelines with respect to this creature, Raya Mira, in either a positive or a negative sense. Nor could my calculating brain link her with any concept of the future, any vision or ambition, like Nanda's hobby room or the photo series with Margot. What I had experienced in the previous half day could not be categorized. It did not inspire me with fear and it gave me no hope.

The brain did not go *bleep*—it lay deathly still, listening to the murmur of the sea behind the dunes and the breathing of a woman on the balcony.

FIVE

Could I have seen it coming? Jelle sometimes said as much. He didn't trust her elusiveness, whereas I had always seen that as an exceptional trait. He didn't trust my trust, for which even I could provide no real foundation. I had no option but blind faith. But then again, I told myself, I'm a pretty level-headed person. Someone who's prepared to face up to the truth, no matter how unpleasant, once it reveals itself to me.

Of course, there's invariably an element of jealousy at play when one friend has found a wife and the other is still wandering around parties and gallery openings on his own. As a rule, though, Jelle and I took turns when it came to the pain and the joys of love, although we sometimes pretended, so as not to hurt the other. This time he saw things differently, and not only because of Raya Mira, whom he still couldn't abide. It was because of me too: the truth was that I was happy and that bothered him.

The good thing about my friendship with Jelle Ripperda is that we both take a somewhat jaundiced view of life. It's been a bond between us since we first met, at St. Ignatius, where we used to organize the cabaret nights for the drama club. It's not that we're pessimistic; we just prefer to look at life from the downside, especially where love is concerned. I've always considered that legitimate: when you've been raised at the bosom of a Yiddish mama, it's pretty difficult to assess other women at their true value. As for Jelle, I always suspected that his suffering was never anything but romantic *Weltschmerz*, the finer points of which he had mastered in German Lit class.

He didn't see it that way himself.

Jelle comes from a well-to-do family: his father is a cardiologist and his mother a nonpracticing psychologist with a passion for interior decorating. It's a shitty marriage, he used to say, but stable. The two often go together. His father was never home, and at least once a year his mother totally redecorated their suburban villa. Maybe he did have cause to be unhappy, but I found that hard to believe. Jelle was used to money. We'd never had any. Jelle had a mother who stayed at home. Mine worked in a drugstore. I did notice that in his eyes girls were always cool and distant, even at St. Ignatius, which was full of sympathetic souls who liked nothing better than a heart-to-heart talk about the situation at home and whether or not you ought to commit suicide.

"My mother's a cold fish," he warned me as we bicycled over to his house. I was going home with him for the first time, to have tea and listen to records. He had the latest Doors record and he said I could borrow it.

His mother was standing in the doorway of a rather grand kitchen. We had already gone through a pantry, swinging doors made of glass, and a vestibule for coats. It was all terribly well thought out: coats on a hanger, purses in a special rack, boots all in a row.

"Gideon who?" Mrs. Ripperda inquired with a penetrating gaze, still holding the hand I had extended.

"Gideon Salomon, ma'am," I replied as I cautiously withdrew my hand. Her grasp was a bit too firm for a first meeting, as if she were researching me. It was something I'd seen before in parents, usually psychiatrists or psychologists. Over a cup of tea they asked you questions you'd really rather not answer, about your parents and girls and how you felt about things.

"Gideon Salomon. How nice, a Jewish boy."

Jelle had told me how she compulsively collected china tea services. She bought them at Metz in Amsterdam and Harrods in London and in Lusaka or Caracas, when Mr. Ripperda was attending some conference or other and she was traipsing around the local sights with the rest of the wives. The way she said it—"a Jewish boy," with an appraising, slightly acquisitive look in her eye—made me feel like a teapot she'd secretly hoped to add to her collection.

Mrs. Ripperda enjoyed being surrounded by the exotic. That was something else Jelle had told me. She organized house concerts, with a pianist from Riga or a singer from Verona, discovered during a junket sponsored by some pharmaceutical firm. Until now there had been no Jews among her acquaintances.

JELLE'S MOTHER WAS always there when he got home from school, to pour the tea and listen to his stories. And while I considered her somewhat peculiar *as a mother*—it was not unusual for her to pick up a magazine while we were having tea and read aloud the specials on curtain material—I did envy him, if only for the teapot. It wasn't the sort of thing we did at home. I was expected to make my own tea (which I didn't, of course), and I spent the rest of the afternoon playing records until my mother got home. And she was always tired.

"But you can hang around school," Jelle said, "or turn up the music real loud, or fry a couple of eggs if you feel like it, without anybody telling you that you're going to spoil your appetite."

"Or smoke cigarettes," I said. I knew that was what really bothered him: the way his mother always noticed everything.

She never reprimanded him; she just asked serious questions, which was even worse. She'd say, "Jelle, I want to have a serious talk with you." About the smell of smoke in his hair, and why he played Joy Division, which was really very depressing music. Once she even asked him why he didn't have any porno magazines hidden under his mattress, like any normal boy his age.

My mother never asked me questions.

AS LONG AS I CAN REMEMBER, my mother got up before any of us. She sat down next to the stove in the living room, drinking black tea with milk in the dusk of the early morning without turning on the light, as if to preserve the nocturnal calm.

I was often awakened by her shuffling around the house. We lived in a small house with thin walls. You get used to it, ignoring most sounds because they've become familiar: the murmured voices coming from your parents' bedroom, the sound of a toilet being flushed, the stove starting up again. These noises become inaudible because of their triviality. But there was always something alarming about her noises. I could tell whether she'd slept well, and what the new day held for us. As in many families, it was my mother's frame of mind that determined the mood of the household. So I awoke with her at the crack of dawn and listened nervously for the sound of a door opening, her step on the stairs, the tick of the teakettle against the faucet. By carefully gauging her morning sounds, I could tell what was in store for me that day.

The living room was separated from the hall by a door with a pane of frosted glass. I used to creep downstairs and look at the figure of my mother illuminated by the light of the stove. I knew her body language better than anyone: the way she cupped her hands around the mug, how she arched her back or sat ramrod straight in front of the stove, the way her feet rested resignedly in her slippers, or bounced up and down like small creatures with a mind of their own. I knew I could open the door and walk into the living room, and she would get up and fix my breakfast and then return to the little stool by the stove, while I sat at the dining room table and finished my toast. But I postponed that moment as long as I could. Being alone with her on the other side of the glass door gave me a sense of power. I could control her by watching her. That way I was always one step ahead of her.

The first transformation in her silhouette came when she heard the sounds coming from the bathroom. My father was awake and had already called my brothers. This was followed by the jostling in front of the bathroom door, and the thump of feet on the stairs as they came down to empty their morning bladders. In a movement that was always the same, regardless of her mood, she got up and went to set the table and slice the bread. First the plates and the mugs for milk, then the knives and the sandwich fixings, and finally the lunch boxes.

My mother always made our sandwiches for us, even when Herman and Geert were already in high school and were expected to repair their own bicycle tires. I always suspected that it was pride that made her go on fixing our lunch; she was determined to continue this form of maternal care, when other manifestations had to be curtailed. Until the year my father gave her an electric knife for her birthday. There was no more sandwich making after that, and the lunch boxes were placed ostentatiously next to our plates.

For years the electric knife lay up in the attic, with the warranty seal still intact. In the end I took it along to school for a bazaar we were having. We got a good price for it, too. It was still in the original box.

After breakfast my mother retired to get dressed. Behind the closed door of my parents' room a second transformation took place, the precise details of which I was never permitted to witness. Once my mother had withdrawn into the bedroom, it was out of bounds. I imagined her as she sat in front of her mirror, put cream on her face, and then powdered it. She never used mascara or eyeliner, but some days there was a touch of blue shadow around her eyes. Then she got dressed. She always wore a dress to the drugstore, and stockings (she could never get used to panty hose), and shoes with laces and a low heel. At the mirror on the landing she did her hair; she always wore an old-fashioned hairdressing cape over her shoulders, so as not to get hair on her dress. And finally she put on a bit of lipstick, just a trace of deep pink, discreet but cheerful. After all, she did work in a drugstore.

When she came down the stairs she wasn't my mother anymore. Her face was the face of the woman in the drugstore: friendly, helpful, inaccessible. Nothing revealed how she had sat there next to the stove that morning. Nothing betrayed that she had fixed my sandwiches. Even the kiss she gave me at the front door was more fleeting than the kiss at bedtime. My mother disappeared, until the moment when she arrived home at the end of the day, when all the operations performed that morning would be repeated in reverse order, and she ended up in the kitchen without lipstick and without the pretty hairdo, in a pair of slacks and a baggy sweater, ready to start the evening meal.

ONE MORNING I was awakened by the light coming through the window. It was late, and yet I hadn't heard my mother. I listened to the ticking of the alarm clock on the other side of the wall; there were no sounds coming from downstairs. I tiptoed down the steps in my bare feet and looked at her chair in front of the stove. It was empty. I walked into the living room and turned the stove up high. Then my father woke up and came downstairs.

"Mama's going to stay in bed today. She isn't feeling well."

He called the store and told them she was sick. My mother was never sick, and I feared the worst. I was hustled upstairs to wake up my brothers. Then I had to help my father with breakfast, since that was something I'd often done together with my mother. He didn't know where to find the chocolate confetti or the butter dish.

That whole day my mother remained behind the closed door of their bedroom. I pretended to be sick, too—that was convenient for my father, because then he could go to work—and offered to take care of her. But at the first knock on the door, she sent me away.

"I really don't need anything, Gideon. Just leave me alone for today."

"Don't you want anything this afternoon either?" I called through the door. I was afraid to turn the handle: I figured the bedroom remained off-limits, even when somebody was sick.

"No, not this afternoon either, sweetheart. I'm just going to have a little nap."

She didn't reappear for another three days. My father slept on the couch and Auntie Ika brought over stew with mashed potatoes and carrots. I was too sick to go to school. For three days I sat on the landing reading comic books and listening at the door for groans. I deliberated about the point at which I could ignore the prohibition and enter her room. I couldn't let her die all alone, without anyone at her bedside! How could my father just go off to work like that? And send my brothers to school, even if they were already in high school? Shouldn't we be holding a vigil, here on the landing? I imagined her in the throes of a horrible death struggle, biting holes in the pillow to keep from making a noise, while I sat there calmly reading Donald Duck comics with a box of cookies on my lap. I knew I would never, never leave my Donald Ducks lying around again, if only that door would open.

The door opened, and there she stood. She looked thinner and had circles under her eyes.

"Shall I make you some tea?" I said, hastily gathering up my comic books.

"First I'm going to see Dad at the office, and then we'll have tea together."

She was already dressed, sort of like the woman in the shop, but not nearly as pretty. She didn't have on any lipstick, and the kiss she gave me was long and warm.

Then Dad went to stay somewhere else. At Auntie Ika's, Mother said. Auntie Ika lived in our neighborhood, but I didn't see his bike in front of her house all the time he was away. That was a couple of weeks, maybe longer. My mother's feet bounced much less during that time.

After my father came back, I looked at her only once more in the early morning. There was something in the way she sat there, something that I no longer understood, and would never understand, no matter how long I looked at her. It was a grown-up thing, something between my mother and my father that was invisible for me.

And yet I will always cherish that image: the figure of a woman in the early morning light, coming to terms with the new day. That I had taken leave of her did not diminish the trust that I had built up. It did not inspire me with fear and it gave me no hope. The image would remain with me forever.

TWENTY YEARS LATER my mother drove her car into a tree. One evening, while my father was watching television, she put on her coat and said, "I'm going out for a while." He probably didn't say anything. I wonder whether he even noticed, whether he didn't just pull up the collar of his cardigan against the draft that entered the living room when she went out the front door.

She took her purse with her, which contained a mirror and lipstick, her house keys, a handkerchief, her wallet with some change, and the snapshots of her sons. She got into the car, turned onto the highway, took an apparently arbitrary exit, and crashed into a tree. It's a pleasant little road, the one she was going down during the last moments of her life. A dark streak in the polder, lined by tall elm trees that rustle even when there's no wind.

Her purse was found by a farmer who was plowing his land. It was lying, unopened, in the rich clay soil. We weren't allowed to see her. There wasn't much left, the doctor said delicately: she wasn't wearing a seat belt.

Bea Salomon–van Geffen, wife of Meep Salomon, beloved mother of Herman, Geert, and Gideon, was killed in a tragic accident, at the age of sixty-four.

That's what it said in the obituary notice. That's the way my father wanted it.

GOING THROUGH HER POSSESSIONS, I found a notebook in the drawer of her desk. Like most women of her generation, my mother had no bank account, didn't own property, didn't have a room of her own. The territory of Bea van Geffen, aged sixty-four, took up less than ten square feet in this world: the space occupied by the walnut rolltop desk she inherited from her aunt, which stood in the sunroom. That's where she had put the notebook, only one page of which was written on, in an old-fashioned, uncertain hand. What was it that she was planning to collect? Memories? Inspiring passages, poems? Was she planning to start a diary, or a long letter?

A single page, no more than five sentences, carefully copied. After that, the notebook was replaced in the drawer. Nothing came of her resolution and no one will ever know what it was.

IT MUST HAVE BEEN a solemn moment. She is alone in the house, the sons have all moved out, and Meep has gone to a meeting. The dishes are done. She dries her hands on her apron and then hangs it on the hook next to the radiator. She makes herself a cup of tea and goes into the sunroom, where the electric stove is already humming softly. She opens the middle drawer and takes out the notebook she bought that afternoon at the office-supply store. It's still in its brown paper bag. The notebook has a dark red cover and delicate blue lines. She opens it, takes out the silver pencil she always uses for her correspondence, turns it until the tip appears, and begins to write:

I Corinthians 13: If I have the gift of prophecy and know all mysteries and all knowledge, yet do not have charity, I am nothing. If I distribute all my goods to feed the poor, and if I deliver my body to be burned, yet do not have charity, it profits me nothing. Charity

*does not rejoice over wickedness, but rejoices with the truth. It bears
with all things, believes all things, hopes all things, endures all
things. Charity never fails, whereas prophecies will disappear, and
tongues will cease, and knowledge will be destroyed.*

EVEN FOR THE BLIND, imagination begins with words.
This thought is not mine; it's a statement by a blind photographer.
He was eleven when he walked into the branch of a tree and lost
his left eye; a year later he stepped on a land mine and was hit in
the right eye. The first photograph he took was the last image that
he saw with his own eyes: a boy standing in front of a mirror with a
Leica in his hand. After that, the lights went out and he started
photographing.

What he photographs does not represent reality, but the landscape of his memory: the bookcase in the house of his grandfather,
who was a rabbi, the little town where he grew up, the orchard
where he lost the sight of his left eye. He explores his object with
his hands and determines how the light should fall. Then he fixes
the image stored in the archive of his memory. The stories of his
childhood are signposts in a world without light.

MY IMAGINATION began with words, too. What had
happened—her death, the tree, a *tragic accident*—had robbed me
of my perception of reality. I once bought a secondhand Mamiya,
a heavy mechanical camera with two lenses, one of which—I later
discovered   had a deviation. I'd never used it It was lying in a
trunk up in the attic at my parents' house. The day after the accident I went upstairs and dusted off the Mamiya. I cycled over to
the provincial highway; it had rained and the furrows in the fields
gleamed with an oily sheen. At the spot where the accident happened I took a photo: a long, straight road, trees on either side,
and the black land all around.

The Mamiya favored me with no more than a row of blurred
elm trees. I left it that way.

Soon afterward my father left home and moved in with the woman we'd known as Auntie Ika twenty years ago, who had long been his mistress. Herman, Geert, and I were allowed to clear out the house and take anything we wanted. The rest was later sold along with the house itself.

I took the mirror that my mother had stood in front of to do her hair. It hung over a dressing table which had a compartment on the top where she kept her brush, a few hairpins, and the pink cape. I took the table too.

Standing in front of the mirror I took a self-portrait with small objects on my tongue: a matzo, a grilled sardine, a piece of lead from her mechanical pencil, a burning match. I did thirteen portraits, the last one with my mouth closed and her hairdressing cape over my shoulders. I printed them in a small format and mounted them in a frame made of natural elm.

In front of her dressing table, with my half-blind Mamiya, I learned to see again.

SIX

How many entrances does memory have? The eyes: they register the image; the brain stores it and—sometime, somewhere—that image can be called up again, although we never really know to what extent it corresponds to the original one. The ears: they make possible the rediscovery of children's songs in a brain ravaged by dementia. The sense of touch: skin recognizes a caress; tongue remembers how nasty sauerkraut tasted, or brussels sprouts. The nose immediately recognizes the house where grandparents lived, or one inhabited by the same smells. But ultimately it is words that activate memory and make recall possible. At least, this is what the scientists tell us. And yet which of us does not cherish some memory that is older than one's own words?

Memory is as layered as a mountain quarry where each deposit is visible. The deepest layers ensure that we do not forget to breathe, even though we do not remember that we must not forget. There are memories that have been declared off-limits: war experiences, the boxing of an ear that resulted in a perforated eardrum. There are memories that resemble an old peat bog in which events are gently cradled and, like a bogman, emerge more or less intact after rocking for centuries in the marshes of oblivion.

Memories are totally unreliable. We forget the greater part of our life, and remember events that never happened. But is memory not the most precious lie one can imagine, because the recall of useless occurrences and trivial details makes the past into a life?

THE OMISSIONS in Raya's memory were grotesque. At first I put it down to reticence. I hadn't known her that long and we used to walk for hours along the beach, talking about our work, our friends, our dreams. She seldom referred to the past, and if it did come up, it was always mentioned casually. She did have a rich store of anecdotes. I interpreted this as discretion. Raya didn't strike me as the type of woman who bares her soul at the first meeting.

"What is your earliest memory?" I asked her. We were talking about our childhood. She comes from a village, while I was born and bred in the city. I firmly believe that the landscape you grow up in determines your outlook on life. You form an image of the world on the basis of what you see when you look out the window: either you're staring at a blank wall or watching clouds scud across the sky. And inevitably that has consequences.

I GREW UP in what was then a new development and is now riddled with concrete decay and scheduled for demolition. Porticoed apartment buildings with storerooms in the cellar and, in between, strips of greenery full of nameless bushes where in our imagination child molesters lurked. Even today I'd recognize those bushes blindfolded, by the musty smell of the street litter caught in their branches and the way the thorns snatch at your clothes when you walk through them.

"My mother had bought me a new pair of pants, dark red corduroy. I was ashamed because they were so babyish and because I was afraid to say anything. Looking back, I guess I was ashamed of my mother's taste and her poverty. I went into a store and stole a pair of jeans. I put them in a plastic bag and hid them in the shrubbery behind the apartment. Whenever my mother decided that it was time for me to wear the red pants, I ran by the bushes on the way to school to change into the jeans. That was a pretty complicated maneuver: I had to find a way to get around my brothers, since the three of us usually walked to school together.

"My guilt ultimately triumphed over my shame. The fact that I had stolen the jeans didn't bother me, but my quick-change performance in the bushes felt like a betrayal. In the end I threw the jeans into a trash can and forcibly ripped my red corduroy pants on the sharp thorns of the bushes. When I got home I showed my mother the torn pants and said I'd had an accident with my bike. She told me not to worry—it could happen to anyone—and said I could pick out a new pair. And then I burst into tears."

"You were born for compromise," she observed. "Was that your earliest memory?"

"No, but it's a nice one." There was so much that I still wanted to tell her. Where do you start?

"I have one, too," Raya said.

I looked at her expectantly, but nothing happened. I thought about the blank wall opposite our balcony and counted my footsteps in the sand. I was at a loss for words.

" W E   C A M E   T O live in the village, my mother and I. It was summer, and I'd just turned seven. After the vacation was over I'd be going to the village school, and in the weeks until then I tried to make friends by hanging around the playground. I was an outsider and it was a closed, almost secretive community. At that time not many people from outside had settled there.

"It was difficult to make contact with the village children. Their accent was one that I found particularly unattractive, and they were always talking about things that I knew nothing about. But what bothered me most was that they were so repulsive: coarse faces, hulking bodies, warts, flat feet—it was as if I had stepped into a painting by Jeroen Bosch. I felt totally out of place. Something had happened in the village shortly before I arrived. The kids didn't give me any of the details, but they made me feel as if they shared something that I was excluded from. They were very self-important about it, which made me feel not only shut out, but also somehow inferior.

"Our next-door neighbor told me that the week before school let out for the summer, a girl had been knocked down and killed, a girl about my age. The class had been to the gym and they were walking back to the school building when she was hit by a truck. Her death had been commemorated by a nice ceremony, the neighbor told me, a service in the village hall and a speech by the principal, and when I arrived at the school in September, there was a photo of her in the hallway, an enlargement of a prayer card: a girl with gaps between her teeth and two blond braids.

"I was the only one in the class who hadn't known her.

"That bothered me. I wasn't interested in the dead girl, or the kids in my class, for that matter, but I realized that I was going to have to get along with them for several years, and it annoyed me that because of the dead girl, the already strong cordon around them had become impenetrable. And they paid very little attention to me, which also stung. After all, I was a newcomer and I felt that this fact alone made me an object of interest. Apparently that was not enough.

"That's what gave me the idea for the story about my dead sister.

"It didn't appear out of the blue. I thought very carefully about how this situation could be turned to my own advantage. I could do something really crazy, but that wouldn't go down very well in the village. I could take up with the biggest hunk in the group, but that idea didn't appeal to me. Then it came to me. I'd give them a taste of their own medicine: I have a sister and she's dead.

"During a long walk across the meadows behind our house, a

dramatic tale took shape: about my little sister who fell off the sidewalk—she was only three—into the path of a car. I worked out all the details: her brains spilled onto the ground, I saw her foot move ever so slightly, and her blue eyes were open. Her overturned tricycle was lying on the stoop. I ran to get my mother and then we were all crying our eyes out and she died in our arms, there on the stoop, and she managed to say 'Mommy' and 'Daddy' and 'Aya'—she couldn't pronounce the 'R'—and then she was dead.

"First I took Jannie into my confidence. I thought she was stupid but she was popular in the group, and I knew she was a terrible gossip, just like her mother. I walked home from school with her, stared straight into the wind and concentrated on my tragic story until the tears came. Jannie wanted to know what was wrong, I turned my face away, she pressed me—as I had hoped—and haltingly I told my story. 'But don't tell anyone. It makes me so sad to talk about it,' I added, as I blubbered into my handkerchief. I knew that if I said it was a secret, my story would get around the village that much faster.

"The next day Mariska asked me if I wanted to play at her house. I said I did. Then came Ilse, a popular girl who had always treated me with the greatest contempt, and after that the other girls asked me if I wanted to join the gym club on Wednesday afternoon.

"No one ever mentioned the story to me except to ask, 'Is it true that your little sister...? And that her brains...?' Then they looked at me with a greedy expression, and I nodded dolefully and I didn't have to say anything else."

WE LAY IN BED under her mother's sheets, yellow and pale green stripes this time, with loose threads at the foot end that your toes caught in.

"Was that your first memory?" I asked.

"It was the moment when I knew for certain that I was a liar," Raya answered.

She looked vulnerable, like a little girl might look who's just moved into the village and is a stranger to the local mores that have prevailed for centuries.

How much of her story was true? She had fallen asleep next to me; the curtain billowed as the sea wind was sucked into the bedroom. I looked at the face and the old hands, lying on either side of her head. Raya sleeps without a pillow; she sleeps on her back with her nose in the air, as if she's afraid of not getting enough air.

How much of Raya Mira was true, and how much was the storyteller in her? Had she told me this to entice me—as she had Jannie—dishing up a story and then sitting back to await the effect?

I thought of her as taciturn, and yet she was good at storytelling and enjoyed it. But after this story, a sneaking doubt began to take shape. I valued her silence more than her words. She knew how to speak, but she didn't talk.

The answer came the next morning.

"It was my first lie," she said with certainty. "I know that for sure. But since then I've never been able to tell which of all my memories are true and which are made up."

What had I wanted to hear? Did I want to be reassured? And why? How true was my own story? Don't I do the same thing, telling only what I choose to remember? Like Raya, I use my memories to present a favorable image of myself, and then hope that's the way she'll think of me.

I tried again. "But what is your biography, for God's sake? The *facts* of your life?"

Please don't let me end up sharing a bed with a character out of a novel, I thought, suddenly angry. Or a congenital liar. Her look made me shiver. Oh, please, not one of those breakfast scenes where the jars of marmalade go whizzing past your ear. Not another female who feels so helpless that she dissolves into tears even before the china starts flying. She looked up from her toast and marmalade. Her glance went over my hands and came to rest on her own hands, which held a cup of coffee. "Will you marry me?" she said.

I went around the breakfast table and knelt down next to her chair, so I could take her in my arms.

SEVEN

SHE TOOK MY NAME even before we got married. Raya Mira Salomon.

"It's so beautiful, more beautiful than anything I could have dreamed up," she said, radiant with joy. Then she started to cry.

She cried a lot then. The swan had died in my arms. She cried when we were lying in bed together; she cried when we made love. She cried when we walked down an elegant shopping street, both of us a bit tipsy, and tried on clothes that we liked but couldn't afford.

"Why are you crying, my girl?"

She knew how to tell stories, but she didn't talk.

"MY MEMORIES BEGIN with you. Everything before that is a story."

The moment had arrived when she would have to come clean. We were sitting in the waiting room at City Hall, clutching a number which guaranteed that in due course it would be our turn to take out a marriage license. In her purse she had a copy of her birth certificate, as I did. We were both nervous. I still wasn't sure whether the whole thing was genuine or a farce. I wanted to marry her, even though I'd known her for only three months and she was a complete enigma. I wanted to reclaim this woman, to cut away layer after layer until I hit the precious lodes. I was not afraid to trust my divining rod, which told me that there was glittering gold beneath the rock. But I also knew that I would have to become the owner first, before I would be given the concession to dig.

"Come on"—Raya was tugging at my arm—"there are twenty couples ahead of us."

I looked up at the electronic display: B322. We were number B343. She dragged me off to a café and ordered champagne.

It was eleven o'clock in the morning. My hair was still wet from the shower.

"Or does this bring bad luck?" She smiled and raised her glass. We toasted.

Oh, my girl, I thought, how disingenuous you are! Let's just drink the day away and weep for what can never be. But not this, not this lie.

"I have something to show you." She dived under the table in search of her purse. "Then I'll tell you a story. This one isn't made up. I promise. And we have to do it now, before it's our turn."

She handed me her birth certificate, a dingy, faded green document. There was an official seal on it, bearing the enormous initials of a Spanish mayor. The rest was illegible. Stapled to the original was the Dutch version. It also had a seal on it, that of a sworn translator. And underneath that was a decree signed by the minister of justice, in the name of the queen.

Annetje Slik, I read, and I looked at her.

"My parents were living in Spain and thought they were happy. My mother comes from Groningen and my father is Spanish. They were married when I was born and then my mother went back to Holland. My mother's name is Gondrina Slik. She wasn't happy in Spain. Not surprising, I guess, when your name is Gondrina Slik and you come from Groningen. She was twenty when she moved back to Holland and went to live with her parents again. That's where I grew up. My parents named me Raya Mira. Here it is. See?"

She showed me the first green paper. I couldn't read any of it; the letters had faded away to nothing.

"When she moved back in with her parents, my mother had me christened Annetje, after my grandmother, in the Reformed Church. She didn't like the name Raya Mira after all. When they were officially divorced, she petitioned the Crown to have my last name changed, too. And the request was granted."

I looked at the papers she had handed me. *Jésus Mendoza, médico*. That's what it said. *Gondrina Slik, ama de casa*. Jésus and Gondrina.

"How did you get these?" I held up the papers.

"I wrote to the registry office in the town where I was born."

"Your mother must have had a marriage certificate. She filed for divorce and then applied to have her daughter's name changed."

"She wouldn't give me the documents. She doesn't want me to get married. It didn't agree with her."

Then Raya began to laugh so hysterically that I was afraid she was having some kind of fit. Call the whole thing off, I thought; this woman's crazy.

I swallowed, almost choked, and then had a coughing spell. Annetje Slik, for God's sake!

"What now?"

Raya ordered a whisky. How about you? No, not for me. You can't blame someone for having been christened Annetje Slik, but I still didn't like it.

"And now I'm going to marry you."

That much was clear.

We probably had less than an hour. I felt in my jacket pocket for the number: B343. I did some quick arithmetic: maybe ten minutes per couple. I'd seen several in the waiting room who had "marriage of convenience" stamped all over them: pimp with whore, mother with the daughter she was marrying off, white male in his fifties with a little Asian thing. If I were the official in charge, I'd be suspicious. And then those foreign birth certificates . . . Let's say, an hour and a half. Time enough to find out whether this concession is worth the investment.

"Raya Mira Salomon—it has a nice ring to it," I said cynically, "in case you ever write a best-seller."

"Just what I was thinking."

Bitch.

She snatched her papers back. "But there's another story."

Go on, Raya. That's your cue.

"So now I lived in the same little town as my grandparents and didn't have a clue what I was doing there. I can't even remember anything about the place. The images in my head are the photographs I used to look at in my mother's scrapbook: Annetje in the backyard sandbox at my grandmother and grandfather's house, Annetje down at the harbor where my grandfather worked, Annetje with the nursemaid who took care of her. I looked and I looked, but nothing of what I saw in those pictures has stuck in my memory. I had wandered into the wrong life: people with whom I felt no affinity, and a landscape in which I would never be at home.

"Imagine: it's flat and windy, and the cows stand with their rumps to the sun. The people are equipped to survive: bony as a cow's shoulder, close as oysters, as if they're trying to protect themselves from the wind, the rain, the wide expanse of sky. The land doesn't live; it survives. It's the same with the people. As young as I was, I couldn't get a handle on it. I was unable to fathom where I had ended up.

"My story begins when we moved to the village. I thought to myself, If I don't feel at home in this life, this landscape, with these people, then I'll make up a story where I do feel at home. I'll make up the story that really is my life."

She drank her whisky like a cup of lukewarm tea. This is a really bad movie, I found myself thinking. But I can't switch channels. Not yet.

"I knew that you don't get very far in this world with a name like Annetje Slik. Don't get me wrong: I'm not blaming my mother. But now that I had a chance to start all over again, I grabbed it. I became Raya Mira. And Raya Mira had a little sister who died under the wheels of a truck, and a father who was there once and then disappeared. I tried it out on Jannie and it worked! I had been given a second chance: I had created a reality that I could get away with."

(OLD HANDS IN dark purple velvet. I'd like to cast you in amber, Raya Mira, here and now—that's how beautiful you are in your desperation. I'd like to immortalize the last few months, mount them on the wall, and seal off time. I want to strip your stories of your voice and fix this face in barite.

Tell your stories, Raya Mira Salomon, again and again, until they fossilize into a memory that you can put into a little box and save.)

"WHAT IS A LIFE, if it doesn't belong to you?" The hysteria had disappeared from her face.

"The first seven years of my life are made up of snapshots and my mother's stories. The next twenty-three years are a book I wrote myself. I'm the author, but not an actor. The story hasn't taken root; it isn't anchored in the memories of the people around me. It's *my* story. I feel at home in it, but I'm alone there."

"Hasn't anyone ever wanted to read that 'book' of yours?"

"Imagination was never high on my mother's list of useful traits. To her I was a dreamer, an eccentric, and my babbling annoyed her. To my teachers I was at best a storyteller, but more often a liar. The Jannies of this world, the Mariskas and the Ilses, they lap it up, but that doesn't help much. They're my audience, the fan club of my melodrama. But a writer doesn't feel a genuine kinship with his readers, or an actor with his audience. You use them to prove to yourself that you've mastered the art. But it doesn't have a lot to do with life."

SHE CRIED UNTIL the morning of our wedding. The alarm clock went off at an improbably early hour, it was dark outside, and the damp cold of the night hung in the bedroom. The searchlight on top of the lighthouse was tracing lines across the sky, and at intervals it illuminated the curtains. In a little while we would be going to City Hall for the ceremony—there was no charge if you got married before nine o'clock in the morning. She lay back against the faded sheets, her eyes swollen. And yet she looked happy. There was a smile breaking through, like when a child takes a tumble but is distracted from the fall even before the pain has ebbed away.

I brought her coffee in bed. "Pretty soon you'll be Raya Mira Salomon."

The tears began to stream again.

The bridal bouquet, a lavender cactus flower, was lying in the linen closet. The stem was wound with ribbons made of the same material as her dress. She wanted to wear purple again, she'd said, and after that she'd throw the dress away. It had served its purpose.

Her tears became a kind of ritual cleansing. She washed away years of untruthfulness, but had to take leave of her lies as well. That was the only prenuptial condition I had insisted on: she was to share memories, so that together we could become a memory, become one story. She had agreed, although she wasn't sure that she wouldn't ever bend the truth again.

"If I marry you, then I have to stop telling lies," she said, pouting.

"No, you don't. As long as you tell me what's true and what isn't."

"*Wahrheit und Dichtung.* Truth versus Imagination."

"Your truth *is* imagination, Raya. But I can get used to that. And you only have to report the out-and-out fabrications."

And she did. In fact, she was so conscientious that I was soon wondering whether I ought to withdraw my condition. I was deluged with notes, which she called *annotations.*

What I just said—that I think you look good in those jeans—that's only true when I'm ovulating. All the other days of the month I think it's your pathetic attempt to look younger than you are. The note lay on the towel. Raya had already gone to bed, and I had taken a shower. We'd gone dancing in the Seventh Heaven.

I think your spaghetti sauce is vile. That one was lying on the counter after dinner, next to the dirty dishes.

But sometimes these communications went into more detail, like after a long walk on the beach when the question came up: which is the bigger lie, writing or taking photographs? Afterward she'd pinned a note to the door of my darkroom:

You recognize my manipulations because you're just as good at bending the truth as I am. The only thing is, you steal other people's stories. You appropriate them in the instant you look through the lens and press the button. You reduce someone else's complex reality to a format that suits you: 2 ½ × 2 ½ inches. The storyteller is more magnanimous. He gives his stories away. Actually, you're nothing but a miserable petty thief. Love, Raya.

S H E   C R I E D   T H A T   M O R N I N G because she knew that she would surrender, give up what she had made of herself in the last thirty years. Alongside the pain of renunciation, there was also a deep and tender emotion, because she sensed that she would find a home that could be shared. Shared by two. And that was probably more than she had ever had.

I asked her why she had never considered taking her father's name. Raya Mira Mendoza. The answer was obvious: she had absolutely no affinity with him. She didn't know her father, or his background. The name Mendoza meant nothing to her.

"Your name, Gideon Salomon, is the name of a man to whom I

have pledged myself. What do I have to lose? Once more I am grafting myself: onto your name, your past, your stock."

T H E   P E O P L E from the Sanitation Department were already at work as we got off the streetcar and started walking in the direction of City Hall. Swarms of gulls circled above our heads as soon as we got close to the little street sweeper that was busily brushing the accumulated muck of the last twenty-four hours out of the gutter. It was just getting light and the city was deserted, except for a few early birds. On the canal we watched as a man who had just parked his car opened his lunch box, peered at the contents, and then rolled down the window and treated the ducks to what his wife had dutifully packed into his lunch box that morning: liverwurst, peanut butter, hard-boiled egg ("He always likes an egg for lunch"). Years of loving care and deadly routine were tossed into the canal and devoured by the ducks.

She had thrown off her old skin. The expression "the most beautiful day of her life" acquired new meaning as I walked at the side of my bride, my future wife. It wasn't the most beautiful day of her life: it was the day that she was at her most beautiful. Stripped of her old skin, not yet adorned with the new one.

EIGHT

We went to see Gonnie Slik, to tell her the news. She knew Raya was planning to get married, but not to whom or when. It was about time I put in an appearance. It was about time Raya showed me where she came from.

The Indian summer of our first acquaintance had turned into fall and there was even a touch of winter in the air. It was raw and rainy, and the sky hung heavy as lead over the land. The landscape of our destination was unknown to me. Raya suggested we take the back roads. We were in no hurry. There wasn't a living soul for miles around, the almost leafless trees surrounding the farmyards stood silent and motionless, and the cows were already in the barn. I couldn't help feeling that any minute I might simply fall off the edge of the earth: the horizon was so solid it was no longer an abstraction, but something concrete—the end of the world. No one can live on this land who wasn't born and bred here, whose roots don't reach deep into the ground, entangled in the old roots of father and forefathers. Anyone else is mercilessly blown away.

Raya sat next to me, looking intently out the window. Once in a while she picked up the tattered dish towel and wiped the window, as if she didn't want to miss any part of the spectacular view. On her lap lay a detailed map of the area. Every time we passed a hamlet, a tumbledown farmhouse, or a row of dike houses, she murmured the name: *Oldorp, Holwinde, Jukwerd.*

She could never live here again, my Raya Mira: she didn't fit into the decor. She was too much of a city dweller. Or no, she wasn't a city dweller—she was uprooted. Perhaps, as she herself claimed, she never had fit into this awesome, inward-looking landscape.

But you can always dream of a land bounded by its own vastness.

I could tell by her restless eyes that she was looking for beacons of recognition.

"I HAD A DREAM LAST NIGHT. I'm bicycling through a deserted village. It's early in the morning, there's no one around, and it's really, really still. The houses look like they're made of cardboard, like a movie set that could fall down any minute. But it's all real. There's a big clock hanging on one of the walls. The second hand is ticking away. The streets are spick-and-span, the houses all painted in the same off-white color.

"I'm cycling along on my Burco, there's a metal basket on the front of the bike, like they use for making deliveries, and in the basket there's a cast-iron frying pan. I have one hand on the handlebars and in the other hand I'm holding a large ostrich egg. I'm cycling very carefully, since I don't want the egg to break before I've reached my destination."

She picked the dish towel up from the floor to clean the window and stared straight ahead, into a void which seemed full of meaning for her, but which had no value whatsoever for me. Often the point of these stories wasn't clear to me. Maybe she was just murmuring words, the way she'd murmured *Oldorp* and *Holwinde.*

"Are you pregnant?" I asked after a while.

"Hey, come on, the dream's not new. I've been having it for years. No, I'm not pregnant, and the egg is not my desire for children."

"Well, what it is then?"

"How should I know?" She turned to look at me. "Don't you think it's a beautiful dream?"

I usually dream about runaway trains and car brakes that fail just as you're careening down a mountain road. The kind of dreams boys have: there's no happy ending but they're not fatal either. I always manage to wake myself up in time.

"Why tell me a dream if you don't want to talk about it?"

"You asked me whether I'm pregnant and I'm not."

"Why tell me the dream?"

"Because it's beautiful."

"Is that all?"

"For Christ's sake, Gideon, how should I know?"

When I wake up from a dream, just before the plane crashes or my speedboat hits the rocks, there's an instant when I'm confused about whether it was a marvelous adventure or an attack of existential angst. But since the latter possibility doesn't appeal to me, I usually opt for the former. That way I can fantasize about what would have happened if I hadn't woken up.

"Do you see that house in the distance?"

She pointed to a small house that stood a little apart from a row of houses beneath the grassy dike. It was white with blue shutters, and struck an improbably frivolous note amid the otherwise sober architecture of the region. No doubt it was occupied by somebody from the city, a writer or artist who hoped to complete his masterpiece in these secluded surroundings.

"That house reminds me of the dream. It's there, it's real, but it seems more like part of a stage set that someone forgot to take down."

"And that makes it beautiful?" I asked cautiously.

"I think it's magnificent. To look at, anyway."

WE FOUND A GUEST HOUSE in a tiny hamlet not far from the town where her mother lived. The slow train hadn't stopped there in years, since the days when the baker did his daily rounds in the village and children's voices could still be heard in the schoolyard. One classroom was now a bank, the other a public health center. The upper floor of the former station had been converted into a guest house, run by the widow of the platform master, who lived downstairs.

From behind the former ticket counter, she carefully noted our particulars in the visitors' book. The gentleman's name. The lady's name. Date of birth. Date of arrival. Length of stay.

"And where are you from?" I could see her thinking: "Not from anyplace around here."

"Married?"

It wouldn't have surprised me if she'd asked to see our marriage license. At long last she took the key from the rack and led the way upstairs. But not before glancing at our luggage and then fixing me with a penetrating look. The message was clear. There was no question of my allowing either one of the women to carry a suitcase upstairs.

"Your room," she said with a broad gesture, as she opened the door of number three. "I don't do breakfasts. Café Beuning in the village opens at seven."

THERE WERE LACE CURTAINS at the windows and several sansevierias, a plant so ugly that I assumed it had long since passed into disuse. The room was dominated by an enormous oak bed, presumably acquired at a public sale of household goods from one of the monumental farmhouses in the area. The little room next to ours had been converted into a bathroom. There was a wobbly shower head from a local do-it-yourself place, and a heavy chest of drawers, no doubt purchased at some other public sale. Because there were no other guests, we appropriated the top of the chest to lay out the remains of our picnic.

Raya settled herself at the table next to the window. The tabletop was covered with a piece of the flowered shower curtain held down with thumbtacks. From our window we looked out over a small housing development that had been deposited in a sunken meadow on the other side of the railroad tracks. In an attempt to join in the spirit of the times, the architects had opted for a ludicrous style that was totally out of place in these surroundings. The doors of the houses were painted in different primary colors, the topsy-turvy dormer windows were screwed onto the roof on either side of the solar panels, and some of the facades were covered in aluminum siding. The net result was a run-of-the-mill Dutch housing development with crooked houses and tiny windows, dangling like a wormlike appendage from the old village center.

I opened the bottle of wine that was left over from lunch and handed Raya a glass. She was sitting at the little table with a special kind of tension in her back that meant that she wanted to start writing.

"I could never live here again," she said, as she gazed at the desolate stretch of land beyond the new housing development. "The landscape appeals to me, but the thought of having to live here is repulsive. The solitude is unbearable."

"And how about your house in the dunes?"

Her house was built into the foot of the dunes. It took up the first floor of a former rope-yard, and the walls were permeated with the smell of hemp and tar. There was a balcony across the full breadth of the back wall, and from there you could look out over a cluster of houses on the edge of the old fishing port. There were still a few cutters moored there, and you could see people mending their nets, but for the most part it was pure folklore. The bulk of the economic activity had moved elsewhere. The enclave was cut off from civilization by the harbors, even though the ferry got you to the center of town in less than fifteen minutes. Living with its back to the land, the community behind the dunes was introverted, and the inbreeding was visible in the faces.

"Somehow that's different," she mused aloud. "Here everything is so *static*. It's a landscape in slow motion. You don't hear the wind because there's nothing for it to blow against. You see the farmer plowing his field, but because of the vastness of the land, you don't see any progression. Every trace of upheaval has faded away."

"Ah, on the coast the foghorn sounds and the tides rise and fall?" I said with a touch of irony.

She turned her face to the spot where I was sitting on the edge of the bed. Oops! That little joke didn't go down well.

"I only live there, Gideon. It's not my life!"

"That's not what I meant," I hastened to say, "but your village-by-the-sea is pretty dull, too."

Her annoyance had dissolved. She was already composing sentences in her head, and I had learned that my lack of understanding was a help rather than a hindrance. I saw her searching for words.

"Here life is nothing but a cycle. All the daily routines are repeated like rituals, over and over, until they automatically acquire significance. Year in, year out: working the land, milking the cows, bicycling into the wind, pollarding the willow trees in anticipation of next year, when they'll have to be pollarded again. That's one way of giving meaning to your life; I realize that. Sometimes the meaning of an act lies in the repetition. But there are other forms of continuity. Less hermetic, less permanent."

She pointed to the bare chestnut tree in the garden of the little station. "Out of its trunk grows a branch, and out of that new branches and burls and chestnuts. Each chestnut is a potential tree, each branch carries a new story, but none of that could have come into being without the old branches, its old trunk, its old root system."

"But that form of continuity always comes to an end. One day the tree dies."

Raya looked at the colossus on which I was sitting. "And then they make a bed out of it that's so strong that it can be handed down from generation to generation."

"Continuity through interruption?"

"No," she mused, "more like an accumulation, where you embroider on what went before. You take with you what you see as valuable; you get rid of whatever bothers you or has already died of its own accord."

"Is that what you wanted to write about?"

"No. I'm thinking of houses."

She turned her back on me and looked out the window. "But maybe it's the same story."

DARKNESS FELL OVER the new development, lending it a touch of that coziness which unwittingly illustrated what Raya was trying to say: the longing for security leads inevitably to stagnation. We watched as, one by one, the lights went on in the houses, here and there the curtains were drawn, and a man came out to take his dog for a walk and exchange pleasantries with a neighbor who also had a dog at his side.

Can a sense of security be significant, more significant than the suffocating certainty of what exists? Can continuity ever escape turning into conservatism?

"Where do you find security, Raya? Does it have to do with houses, or with your memories?"

Raya turned to face me, her dark eyes blind for what they saw: blind for the big old-fashioned bed, for the flowered wallpaper, blind for me, her husband. This is what Socrates must have looked like just before his death: eyes that survey an internal landscape.

Eyes are not the mirrors of the soul, it suddenly occurred to me. They are mirrors of passion, something that goes even deeper, something that is even more ungovernable than the soul.

"That egg," Raya said. "It has something to do with that egg, doesn't it?"

SHE SAT ACROSS FROM ME, Gonnie Slik, having sunk ponderously into the large leather couch, and sipped from her glass.

"So you're still living alone?"

I had given her the announcement, the card we sent to our friends to let them know that Raya and I were married. It had both her address and my address on it. We hadn't found a house yet. The mother looked at her daughter, who was sitting on the hassock in front of the fake fireplace. Raya looked away, as she had from the moment we turned onto the street where Gonnie Slik lived. She knew the place well: it was the street of her childhood. After Raya's grandparents died, Gonnie had moved into the house she'd grown up in. It was a modest redbrick home with a smallish garden full of old-fashioned plants like rhododendrons, a sour cherry, and an ancient Juneberry bush. Her mother was waiting for us in front of the house, with her winter coat slung over her shoulders and a scarf around her head. The coffee she served us later tasted as if it had been made a long time ago, and there were pastries on the table. But the reception we received was odd. I could see how she was straining her eyes as the car turned onto her street, and how she hesitantly raised one hand. But then she went back into the house and closed the door behind her.

"Don't you want to go around back?" I said a few minutes later as Raya headed in the direction of the front door, which was still firmly closed.

"Of course not. It's not my house."

She rang the doorbell and her mother opened the door, as if she hadn't been standing in the front yard a minute ago, waving to us. Her coat and scarf were hanging on the coatrack, and her lipstick had been recently applied. She shook hands with Raya and kissed her on both cheeks, and then rushed off to the kitchen to put our flowers in a vase. Up until then not a word had been spoken except for a "Well" (the mother) and an uncertain "Yes" (the daughter). I couldn't manage to say anything. She hadn't put out her hand, due to sheer awkwardness, I guessed, but she had looked at me.

"You're still living alone, Annetje?" said the mother again, in the direction of the uncommunicative creature

opposite her. In the previous five minutes Raya seemed to have re-
gressed some twenty years. She sat there like a stubborn child who
couldn't quite decide whether she should be angling for her
mother's love, or screaming out her loathing.

I gave it a try. "Raya's put her house up for sale. We're looking
for something with a garden. For the two of us."

"How nice. For the children!" Gonnie leaned forward, visions of
grandmotherhood dancing in her eyes. How bored she must be, I
thought, alone in this house, in this godforsaken town.

"Jesus, Mother, all we did was get married!" Raya reacted as if
she'd been stung by a wasp.

"Yes, why did you actually?" her mother asked.

It didn't strike me as a stupid question. As far as I knew, Raya
had always been fiercely independent, and I could understand how
a mother might feel the need for some explanation. Raya got up
from the hassock and went over to the window to look at the garden, where the witch hazel was timidly coming into bloom.

"I brought Gideon to meet you, Mother. I thought you might
want to get to know him."

(I   s e e   a   c h i l d   in the door opening of the kitchen. Her
mother is standing at the counter, peeling potatoes. The knife
makes a scratching noise when it hits a chunk of clay attached to
the potatoes. *Plop, plop, plop,* they drop into the pan of water standing in the sink. Outside, a light rain is falling, and it's getting dark.
The little girl has been working on a drawing at the dining room
table. Now she's standing by the kitchen door, unnoticed by the
mother, absorbed in her own thoughts.

"Mother," the child says cautiously, "I made a drawing. Would
you like to see it?"

She holds up the piece of paper. The mother turns her head
ever so slightly, while her hands go on peeling the potatoes.

"Yes," she says, and turns back to her work.)

RAYA TURNED AWAY from the window. "We're leaving."

She finished her coffee and walked to the door. The pastries on the table were untouched. I looked at the mother and saw a smile cross her lips. With growing amazement I had observed these two women, who appeared to have nothing in common except the game they were playing. Beautiful, dark-haired, restless Raya, and Gondrina Slik, stout, graying, and resigned in a corner of her leather couch. Was this wisdom or cruelty? What kind of mother was this?

Maybe this is what there is between a mother and a daughter, always and everywhere: you're so close to each other that it itches and grates.

When I got to the door, I looked back. Gonnie Slik was still sitting on the couch, looking straight ahead. An echo of that smile lingered around her mouth. Her hands rested in her lap.

Old, ruthless hands.

WE STOOD ON TOP of the dike and looked out over the mudflats. I pointed my crippled Mamiya alternately in the direction of the water and the land behind the dike on which we were standing. I bent over the camera, which held out the promise of results I knew it couldn't produce.

"Is it sea that's fallen dry or submerged land?"

I didn't expect an answer and I focused on a shot of the water, crowded out by the land. Flood gave way to ebb. From some distance I heard the sound of Raya's voice: " 'Like playing with water itself, playing with the thought that you will one day at last know what it is. It has been rain, a river, a sea—here it was, here I saw it—and I see water and do not know what it is.' "

"What's that?" I asked.

"A poem by Rutger Kopland," she said.

"He's right," I remarked, "we're looking at it and we still don't know.

"It's better to love it than fight it to the death." She turned back to the land. Behind the dike, the water was high in the drainage ditches, and the second dike rose up in the distance. And beyond that, the church towers on clay mounds.

"Are you talking about the water," I asked, "or your mother?"

"For a long time it was my mother: playing with the thought that you will one day at last know what it is. I don't know, and I don't think I'll ever find out. I'm her daughter, and that says it all."

"You're not a mother yet. That makes a difference."

"That makes a difference," she echoed. "Sea that's fallen dry, or submerged land—it's two worlds and yet one. For now, I'm standing on the dike and I'd prefer to keep my feet dry."

BACK IN THE CAR, I thought back to the dream about the egg, the new housing development, the empty desolate land, and her mother. I thought about my wife and looked aside at her cautiously, for in spite of herself, there sat Annetje, too: the beauty of Spain, the inflexibility of Groningen, my silent liar.

"What was your destination, Raya? Where were you going with the frying pan and the egg?"

"Ah, my darling, that's the question I've been waiting for."

NINE

WE GOT MARRIED in the fall of 1990, three months after we met at Christian Winkler's. Shortly afterward she found a house just outside the city center. It was small, but it had a garden. Her dune house was sold, I gave up my rented apartment, and we moved into the house that belonged to both of us.

Winter came, and Raya was carrying our daughter.

The purple dress didn't end up in the trash can, after all. Raya got out the sewing machine and made two small dresses out of it, one for summer and one for winter. She was certain it would be a girl. The winter dress had sleeves and the summer dress was embroidered with the ribbon from her bridal bouquet.

Raya quit her job at *Fisheries Bulletin*, the magazine that had provided her with an income for the past few years. There was more and more demand for the work I was doing with my Mamiya, and we decided that for the time being we would live solely on my income.

ON AUGUST 31, 1991, our daughter was born, Lizzy Mira Salomon, a month early, during a summer storm. Raya withdrew even further and wrote short stories for literary journals, most of which didn't last very long. But she never actually broke through. For the money, she occasionally wrote a piece for her fisheries magazine; this also gave her the feeling that she wasn't totally cut off from the world. She even considered signing up for an intensive teacher-training course, but after a bit of fieldwork at local high schools, she thought better of the idea.

WE DID NOT SEE Gonnie Slik again. She sent us a Christmas card, and after the birth of our daughter a large box arrived with Raya's own baby bed, complete with embroidered sheets, folded between layers of tissue paper. There was also Annetje Slik's scrapbook, the record of Raya's first seven years of life.

The shipment also contained a box of cuttings. We didn't know what they were, but they had twigs and roots and leaves. During our visit to her mother, Raya had remarked on how old the Juneberry bush had gotten; she was hoping for a young shoot. They turned out to be rhododendron cuttings. Nevertheless, Raya cared for the young plants with great solicitude.

2

Feel

TEN

WHEN DOES AN EVENT become a memory? When does a memory become a story?

I remember each detail of her death, but so little of her life. We are complacent, not to say arrogant, in failing to engrave upon our minds all that is dear to us. But we do not take the trouble to remember something that we fully expect will be repeated tomorrow: how many slices of toast she had for breakfast, and what her favorite dress was.

Did she suck her right thumb or her left? Did she already know how to read? What were the names of the seven stuffed animals she always took with her to bed?

She laughed a lot—at least that's how I remember her. But did she actually laugh a lot? Perhaps I recall her fits of helpless laughter while she was brushing her teeth because they were rare, because by and large she was a rather serious little girl?

She had green eyes and Raya's black hair. She had lost her first milk tooth. She was into gymnastics. She always had bruises all over her body, and dirt held an irresistible attraction for her. She enjoyed painting more than drawing. She hated to have her nails cut, but could sit there for hours having her hair brushed. She was pretty, and not only in our eyes. The photographs provide confirmation— and I wish I'd taken more of them.

How many pictures do we have of Lizzy—the ordinary snapshots of her under the shower or being read to, or during the public gymnastics lessons? I didn't look carefully enough during those unguarded moments; otherwise I'd have seen that ultimately they would be the most important images of all: details of a life that once existed, but whose importance I failed to see.

Her face, I remember her face. But her life escaped me, even before it ended.

I KNOW HOW IT SMELLED on the morning of August 31, 1996, the fifth birthday of our daughter, Lizzy Mira Salomon. We had kept all the doors and windows closed that night, because there was a storm coming. We had heard the weather report on the radio as we lay in bed, and had gotten up again to take the necessary precautions. It wasn't raining yet, but all day long the atmosphere had been crushing, and the wind was already tugging at the window frames.

The house was decorated with balloons and paper garlands. The layers of meringue I'd made the previous evening were standing on the counter. Tomorrow I'd use them to build Lizzy's birthday cake, alternating the meringue layers with custard and lots and lots of strawberries with sugar.

Lizzy loved strawberries with sugar. I remember that.

I know that Raya went outside to put the lawn chairs under the overhanging roof. I know that I went into the room where my daughter was lying asleep, checked to see that the window was bolted, and then covered her bare back with the white sheet.

I know that even our bedroom window, which is usually wide open, was only cracked that night. The weatherman's warning was clear enough: the storm was going to hit the country with hurricane force.

I know that I shut the door to the hall.

I know that after that we went to sleep.

WHEN I WOKE UP that morning the house was hot and stuffy and there was a penetrating, slightly sweet smell in the air. I opened our bedroom window, but that brought no relief. In the hall I started to feel uneasy; the strange smell was so pronounced that I found myself gasping for breath. And yet I went on through to the kitchen and opened the back door. The foliage had held up pretty well during the night, and I know I was surprised that the garden had come through more or less unscathed. I don't know what I'd expected to see: the backyard transformed into a battle scene full of mud and broken branches? Shrubbery flattened by the onslaught of nature? The air was clear and cool in my nostrils, after a stuffy night of restless vigilance.

I know that I put the kettle on, that I sniffed the aroma of coffee as it absorbed the boiling water, and that I had no desire to investigate the source of the ominous smell hanging in the air.

I know that I was surprised that Raya wasn't up yet. It was early morning, but her coffee mug was still upside down in the dish drainer, and the chair on the deck was wet from the rain that had come slanting under the overhanging roof. The house was as untouched as if it had stood empty during a long absence. Stale air.

I know that in the end I went into Lizzy's room, carrying a cup of hot coffee. The door of her room was ajar, a sneaker wedged between door and doorpost to keep it from closing all the way: we knew from experience that this was guaranteed to banish nightmares and scary thoughts. As I pushed the door open with my shoulder—carefully, so as not to spill the coffee—my hand automatically slid across to the light switch next to the door, to turn off the hall light. It was already off. Raya must have gotten up without my noticing, since we had promised our daughter that the hall light would stay on until all three of us were awake.

HER ROOM IS BATHED in the bluish glow of early morning. The light filters tentatively through the organdy curtains, highlighting the white of the sheets below the window frame. Raya is sitting in a corner of the bed. She is leaning against the wall. The long, black hair hangs limply on either side of an ashen face, her bathrobe is hanging open, and on her lap, against her bare breasts, lies Lizzy. She is wrapped in a sheet, like an oversize baby, an under-sized Christ, one small, pale foot visible, the other concealed by the bed linens.

They sat there like the perfect Pietà, the image Michelangelo must have seen in his mind's eye: a woman, neither desperate nor resigned, clinging in total devotion to a child she has already given up, as she cradles the body in her arms.

I knew: she is dead.

LIZZY'S SKIN WAS LIKE MARBLE, although it wasn't cold. I stroked the tiny black hairs on her forearm and tried to re-call whether Michelangelo had thought of them, those hairs on the forearm that stand on end when startled, even on marble skin.

"Did she have a BM?"

I didn't know what to say. I knew that it would reassure me to know where the smell came from which had bothered me for the last fifteen minutes. I sensed that the explanation would contain the answer to the question I couldn't ask.

I nestled down next to Raya. The sheet in which Lizzy was wrapped was saturated with excrement and I smelled the unreal smell of a child's body that had emptied itself: a smell that sud-denly was no longer alarming, or unpleasant, or dirty, but tender and precious. It was the last visible, tangible thing our daughter had left behind for us.

Again I looked at the foot that dangled, lifeless, between sheet and bed. It was pale and transparent and perfectly formed. Her little toe was a triangle that leaned in perfect harmony against the second toe, which had a tiny hollow to make room for the third, and so on, cozily snuggled one against the other, right up to the big toe. The arch was curved and smooth, surrounded by a rough ring of callused skin that continued right to the heel bone. The nail on her big toe appeared to be torn and was slightly ingrown. Her feet bore witness to a life; they had carried her for five years. She had traveled on wings, and yet her feet were callused. Like a true mortal child.

T H E F O O T of the Pietà is dulled by the many caresses, the toes have been rubbed away, stroked by thousands of passersby searching for faith, love, hope—whatever it is that we believe we are lacking in this earthly life.

I looked at my daughter's feet. They were perfect. The toes and the nails and the skin were all there. I hadn't stroked her enough while she was alive. I took the foot in my hand and began to stroke it. I wanted to stroke it until it fell apart. Until it faded. Until it became warm. Until it began to shine.

ELEVEN

We tell ourselves lies about immortality, because you can't live without the certainty of a tomorrow, even though you know that it's a gamble, a lucky break, if that tomorrow really comes. We lie to ourselves about immortality because without that there would be no love, no science, no procreation, no war. Death may be the driving force, but without the illusion of immortality we are left empty-handed in this life. No, the true lie is not immortality, but the conviction that we could somehow play a role in it.

That we have a say in things.

That our life could possibly belong to us.

It was Saturday night, August 30, 1991. Raya was asleep, in the bed that had already been placed on blocks, just to be on the safe side. Strictly speaking, the birth of the child was not imminent—Raya's due date wasn't until the twenty-fifth of September, almost four weeks away—but that evening she had announced that it would be a Sunday's child and would be born tomorrow. Her pelvic bones were beginning to open up, she said. She couldn't keep it inside her any longer.

She'd been sitting at the table writing, legs apart, a pillow in the small of her back, with a glass of red wine in her hand and a cup of green tea on the table to dilute the alcohol. She hoped for the best, as she had for the past eight months.

As she looked up from her notebook I saw a change in her face, subtle but unmistakable. At first I was elated: a miracle was taking place before my eyes. I was witnessing the birth of a mother! But then I caught myself. It was something else: I saw my Raya Mira slipping away into a universe that was foreign to me. It occurred to me that this is what someone who was dying might look like. In retrospect there was perhaps more truth in this than I was prepared to admit. My wife was dying and in her a human being was being born, one who carried a desperate responsibility which I could not yet even begin to fathom.

She tore the page she had just finished out of her notebook. "For you," she said, as she handed me the sheet of paper.

I read what she had written with a growing sense of alarm. It didn't seem to me the sort of thing a mother-to-be should be thinking about on the evening before she was to give birth. "And the birth of a child may well be the biggest lie of all," she said when I looked up from the paper. She settled herself next to me on the couch. Her belly was as taut as a basketball.

"Let's just wait and see, shall we," I joked cautiously.

"I want to stay on top of it, Gideon. I don't want it to take me by surprise."

She'd gotten up again and was looking out the window of the sunroom, staring into the black night. The blue shirt of mine she was wearing formed a sloping diagonal over her breasts and her belly. It is a centuries-old silhouette, the greatest conceivable cliché: the image of a heavily pregnant woman against a black background. And yet I had to fight off the urge to reach for my camera.

"What are you afraid of, my girl?"

The answer was long in coming. I was used to her silences. In a sense, they even reassured me. There was less chance of a lie.

"Bearing a child," she began tentatively, "no, making a child is the ultimate attempt to exorcise our mortality. We try to fool time and death and decline by implanting our genes in new flesh. But in doing so, we are actually hastening our own death."

"What do you want to stay on top of, Raya? You're going to have the baby tomorrow, you say. Isn't that enough?"

"The pain of childbirth—I don't think that's what I'm dreading. Half the people on earth have gone through it, and in the end most of them have survived. But the confrontation with your own inadequacy, Gideon, tomorrow, when that tiny creature is lying in your arms..."

After that it was quiet for a very long time. An enormous sadness had come over me, because I realized that the watershed was a fact. The memories that we were going to write together—the only prenuptial condition that I had imposed: don't lie to me!— had come to an end. And damn it, the cause of the break between us was a lie. But one that neither of us had foreseen.

Raya pointed to the crib, which had been tucked out of sight behind the boxes in the sunroom. "Tomorrow, my dear Gideon, the tragedy of human failing will be lying there."

AFTER SHE'D GONE TO BED I sat down on the couch. I poured myself a large glass of wine and—uncharacteristically— lit a cigarette. Then I cried and yelled until I had no voice left. Tomorrow it would be her turn to scream and rage her way to motherhood. For me the pain of labor had already begun.

SHE'S SMALL, much smaller than I thought a baby would be. I can hold her in the palm of my hand, and her tiny feet don't even reach to my elbow. She has her eyes closed. I want to know whether they're brown or blue, but all I can see is a delicate membrane no bigger than the nail on my little finger, stretched over the eyeball and quivering slightly. Her hair is long and dark, and she has a fine line of black, silky fluff running down her back, all the way to her tailbone. At the very end, in the little cleft just above her buttocks, the fluff comes together in a tuft, a tiny bit of fuzz. Would she have a tail? Would she always have that fuzz at the end of her spine, in the cleft above her buttocks, as a souvenir of her fetal existence?

Raya has no fuzz at the bottom of her spine, but she does have dimples in her buttocks. Maybe the baby will have dimples in her buttocks, too. Maybe she'll be blond. Maybe she has blue eyes, like mine, or brown, like Raya's. What is it that determines eye color? I know we had it in high school biology: XX plus XY means blue, or maybe the other way around.

The maternity nurse has wrapped her in linen: she looks like a papoose, wrapped tightly from top to toe in cotton diapers, with just the tip of her nose peeping out from under a little hood. Her wrinkled skin has been rubbed clean. The tiny hands are those of a dying woman: transparent, the veins visible. And I think to myself, If I hold her hand up to the light, I can see the bones, take an X-ray picture. I can feel that there are bones inside, matchsticks joined by little knobs. At the end of each finger there's a match head, pale pink, almost white. And another one at the end of each toe: even smaller, but unmistakable.

"Please close the window," I say to the nurse. The baby has been weighed and found wanting, and when I look at her I think, She could easily blow straight out the window. The terrible storm of the previous night has receded; outside the sun is shining mercilessly, the windows at either end of the house are open, and still the hot air hangs solid as a rock between the four walls. Four weeks premature, too small, underweight and yet perfect. With black hair and eyelids and nails and bones and a wound that would later become a navel.

She can stay; she's strong enough. And it's warm outside.

Raya's big, empty belly is lying next to her like a stranded whale. She has turned onto her side and the baby is drinking from her breast. The large body has served its purpose; the small one is not yet ready to face life. For now, they are doomed to togetherness.

I drape a clean white sheet over them, the smell of laundry powder fills the house, the washing machine is churning out load after load, and in the kitchen the maternity nurse is fixing strawberries and whipped cream, and coffee for the family doctor, who'll be by in a little while. The midwife and her assistant are talking in low voices with Raya, about cracked nipples and engorgement and stitches, and the color of a baby BM (greenish at first, then yellow to mustard-colored).

"The entire wall of the uterus is an open wound, Raya, where the placenta has torn away. But the bleeding is red and clear, and that's a good sign."

Blood and milk and BMs and laundry powder and strawberries and whipped cream.

"Is it all right if I go out for a while?"

I don't know to whom the question is addressed. Or why I find it necessary to ask for permission. Around me I see a vague nodding of heads. The women have other things on their minds.

I shut the door behind me.

I'm NOT SURE what I expected, but not this: a day like any other day. In a daze, I walk down the same street I walked down yesterday and the day before yesterday, past the same houses and gardens I see day in, day out, whenever I go out to mail a letter or do an errand. The trees look the same as always, though they lost a lot of their leaves during the past night. I look at the faces of the people passing by. It surprises me that they don't notice anything about me, no sign of recognition. We walk past each other, like any other day.

I must reclaim this terrain. I must reclaim myself. I have a daughter. My wife is a mother. And I am now a father.

"LIZZY IS HER NAME. Lizzy Mira Salomon."

She was wearing the purple dress that Raya had made for her, with the long ribbons from the bridal bouquet wound three times around her waist. Her black hair had fallen out. At five weeks, she was tiny and bald. Her eyes inclined toward dark, but we couldn't be sure: Lizzy slept away the hours she'd missed out on in the womb.

That evening was a celebration: we drank to the fact that the child had survived the first few weeks of life and was being weaned from her mother.

We invited our friends over and presented the baby to them. Conscious of the drama of the moment, Raya entered the living room with the child in her arms, radiant as a Madonna. She was so beautiful, my Raya Mira, in her white lace dress, proud that after only a month her flabby belly was gone, proud of the huge breasts that filled her décolletage. Even the dark circles under her eyes had temporarily disappeared and the cracks in her fingers were invisible. For now, she surrounded herself with her personal scents: hair spray and smoke and freshly washed clothes. Our child was given a name and a place of her own in this life, and Raya and I picked up the thread of our lives, in the intimacy of a gathering of friends.

Jelle was there, with his new girlfriend. She introduced herself as Birgit Bijvoet, a nutritionist, and she had sandy hair, just like Jelle, and lots of freckles. I found myself imagining what their child would look like, with skin that flushed easily and glasses with lenses that were just a bit too thick.

That's what happens when you become a father: you start noticing things like that.

In a corner of the room stood my brothers, dour as farmers' sons, each holding a glass of beer. I went over to them.

"Aren't you going to ask me what it's like to become a father?"

No one had ever asked me what it was like to have a child. Not my brothers or my father, not even my friends. But of course they hadn't asked me any questions: as long as it doesn't involve them personally, the matter is of no importance. Back when I was one of them, I had no more sympathy than they did for the people who stand at a bus stop fumbling with their trendy buggy, because they've just discovered that buggy and baby won't go through the automatic doors at the same time. I used to look at them the way I looked at the mandrills in the zoo: a species not to be envied for the fate to which they had been condemned.

But things were different now. I had joined the guild of mandrills. A wave of loneliness came over me.

"And what would you say if I did ask?" Herman stood there grinning. By that time he had progressed to a new guild, that of the weekend father. The odd one-night stand, sometimes a stayer in his bed, but never for longer than a couple of breakfasts. I got the impression that he was enjoying life.

"Do you remember what it was like," I asked, "the first couple of weeks with your child?"

Herman had never spent so much time at the office; that's something I did know.

"No," he admitted, "I don't remember, and I don't want to remember."

C U R I O S I T Y. If there was one thing that impelled me homeward at the end of the day, it was curiosity. Not love—I didn't know her. She was foreign to me. Home had become foreign to me. A thousand helping hands ruled over our house: the maternity nurse, girlfriends, Raya's own capable hands. I had become superfluous. I had done my work. A thousand hands had taken over, and still I could not let go. My curiosity was too strong: about the color of her eyes, about her voice, about her preferences in this life, about her name. Whether in the end the name that we had chosen for this little girl would fit her like an old winter coat you can't bear to part with.

And so I came back home every day, curious about what she would become. Not about what she was.

That's what I told Herman. But he was so drunk that none of it registered with him. He grinned amicably in the direction of the silk-screen print on the wall behind me.

"Prolactin," said the woman next to me, who had apparently been following the conversation. It was Birgit, the nutritionist.

I was totally bewildered. "Prolactin." I am surrounded by idiots, I thought.

Birgit smiled at me with compassion, as if this revelation was meant to be reassuring. "It's a female hormone that stimulates the milk production. We know from studies with monkeys that it's also produced by males during their mate's pregnancy. Which explains why most men 'stay on the nest,' so to speak. Even though they're totally useless," she added with a laugh.

"Are the fathers really useless?" I asked her.

"You can say that again," Herman boomed next to me. I wanted to ask him who he was thinking of: our father or himself. But his grin had already wandered to the bookcase.

"Yes, in a sense they are useless," said Birgit, as she reached for Jelle's arm.

I looked around for Raya. She was leaning against the door of the sunroom, and looking outside. October: the monsoon had begun.

"Are you having fun?" I asked.

Her silence conveyed doubt.

"Aren't you having fun?"

"Oh, I guess I just don't know what to make of all this." She gestured in the direction of the living room: "I'm so happy that everyone's here, but it's as if I'm not really here myself."

"Then where are you?"

She motioned with her head in the direction of the junk room, which had been transformed into a nursery.

"But isn't that exactly what you are today? Big Mama?"

I gathered her into my arms. I felt the resistance of her breasts, still used to nursing, and her nipples hardened at the touch of my body.

"Are fathers useless?" I asked, as I buried my nose in her hair.

"How should I know?" The answer came just a bit too quickly. I saw that this startled her. "But what I am, I could never have become without you."

She kissed me and wriggled out of my embrace. "Come on, let's play charades!"

WHILE A GROUP of more or less inebriated guests threw themselves into the game ("Gag!" "No, gate, grate." "Gregarious... gaga, that's it!" "No, it's Gagarin." "What's a *gagarin*?" "Who knows what a gagarin is?" "That doesn't count. She's right—that one doesn't count."), I walked out into the night. A pale mist rose from the black earth. Raya had started preparing the garden for winter. She didn't know exactly what this entailed, but she'd read somewhere that it was very important. All the plants that she didn't immediately recognize were thrown into the trash can for organic waste. She said it couldn't do any harm. The usual stuff would come up in the spring, whether we wanted it to or not.

The soil—sterile and useless—was soaking up the rain. In the background there was the plunk of raindrops falling on leaves, merging with the other drops and, larger now and heavier, continuing their fall. At the end of the garden the fog hovered just above the peat like swamp gas or the eerie mist that people call the white witches, in which real witches live and dead souls who lost their way in the bog come to life again. Raya once told me that the village people never went out when the white witches hung over the land. They lured you into the bog and you never came back.

"What are you thinking about?"

I was startled by the soft voice next to me.

"White witches," I replied, and could have bitten off my tongue.

It was Brechje standing next to me, a friend Raya had known since she first arrived in the city. They had roomed next door to each other in the student dorm. Brechje Kalma was a physics major and an albino. She was milky white without a trace of color or freckles: her strawlike hair, her eyelashes, and her eyebrows were all white. She wore dark contact lenses and was all but blind. She was most comfortable at night, and that was how the two of them had met: for weeks Raya had been awakened by one of her house-mates who made a habit of getting up in the middle of the night to fry eggs at the kitchen unit in the corridor. One night she stormed out of her room to voice her annoyance. And, as Raya later re-counted amid general hilarity, there stood Brechje in a shapeless nightgown, frying eggs in the blue glow of the gas flame. There was no light on in the kitchen—Brechje couldn't see anything anyway—and all Raya saw was a "fluorescent" nightgown with white hair and red eyes. "Jesus!" she said with a gasp, "you look like a witch."

Brechje had burst out laughing and invited Raya back to her room for a mug of tea. It was the middle of the night, and they be-came friends.

"WHITE WITCHES, RIGHT?" She smiled. She put her arm around me and whispered in my ear, "Shall I take you away from this slough of merriment, and carry you off to the morass, where everything is warm and still and calm? Come on, give the witch a kiss."

I rested my head on her shoulder for a minute and then looked back in the direction of the house. Through the sunroom window I saw Raya fluttering around the room in her white dress, acting out some word. The others watched, frowning, laughing, gesturing drunkenly in the direction of the black window. I saw them shout-ing out words to Raya, who flew up against the bookcase, felt the wall, and then came to rest in the light of the lamp.

A moth, I thought.

"What do you see?" asked Brechje.

"*Mutter Courage und ihr Kinder.*"

"Brecht? Is she doing Brecht?"

"No, she's doing Raya."

"She's lovely."

"Well, she really did her best tonight."

"No—well, yes, Raya too. I meant Lizzy. She's lovely."

"How would you know? You can't see a damned thing."

Brechje had never seen her handicap as a problem She didn't wear glasses because it wouldn't have made much difference. She was skilled in braille.

"Her skin feels good. And her head, the shape of her head is lovely."

There was a terrible racket coming from the house, followed by roars of laughter. I looked around. Raya was sitting on the floor, her head bleeding, with the shattered remains of the Tiffany lampshade lying in her lap, and she was helpless with laughter. Hands came to her rescue. Brechje and I went into the kitchen.

"What happened?"

"The moth just crashed," I said.

THROUGH THE HALF-OPEN DOOR of her room, I heard a soft whimpering sound. The racket had woken Lizzy up. In the kitchen Raya stood with her head under the cold faucet. A stream of red water fell onto the dirty dishes in the sink. Brechje's white hands were resting on her shoulders as Jelle searched the bottom of the kitchen cabinet for a dustpan and brush. I closed Lizzy's door behind me and looked at the tiny doll lying in a bed that was much too big for her. I lay down beside her and stroked her head. It's beautifully shaped, Brechje had said, but what is a beautiful shape? It reminded me of a quince, round and deep pink and tapered at the top. She had a pointed forehead. Her hairless skull had a dent in the middle, where the fontanel was in the process of closing. The mouth was fine and sharply outlined, as if it had been drawn with a pencil. Her cheekbones were wide apart. She looked at me with dark wet eyes: dark but colorless, with pouches, just like her mother.

"It's not easy, getting used to life," I told her.

She took my finger in her hand and held it tight. I put my nose in her neck. She didn't smell human yet, more like sweet rolls.

Then a large, silent yawn issued from the toothless mouth. She sighed deeply, and fell asleep.

What is to become of her? I thought: such a tiny, vulnerable creature, and so many dragons on her path. If it's not the white witches, then it'll be the Johnnies and Mustafas coming to get her. And what am I supposed to do? What do I do until then?

Sleep tight, Lizzy; then you'll grow big and strong and brave. Then Daddy will be able to sleep soundly again. And then there'll be another new day.

TWELVE

THERE MUST HAVE BEEN a day when I decided I was going to love her. I don't remember exactly, but it was probably during one of the many nights, at the beginning of her life, when I lay next to her on the bed and gazed at that face, so much a part of me and yet so foreign. I longed for the skill to paint or sketch my daughter, to get closer to her, to study her, to make her mine.

I didn't know her, and the father in me was also a stranger.

Raya maintained that love is forged by caring for a child, as opposed to gazing at her for hours on end. But to me that was a cop-out: if you wipe enough bottoms, attachment will automatically grow. It sounded more like a commercial for diapers, and it surprised me that Raya had fallen for it, that myth of parental love.

"It's not a myth," she insisted. "It's true of every single thing you do. The devotion and care and concern you put into it—that's what determines the pleasure it gives you."

"And what about love?" asked the doubting Thomas.

"It grows under your hands; it comes of itself, in time."

AH, RAYA could be very emphatic in her assertions.

When we moved into our new house, she decided that we needed a new floor. The parquet floor bequeathed to us by the previous occupants was still in excellent condition, but it wasn't "her" floor.

She didn't want to become attached to a floor which bore the imprint of someone else's life.

"You don't think you're being just a wee bit superstitious?" I found her conviction touching, but extravagant.

"Okay, I admit it's time-consuming," she said, with a nice sense of understatement, "but if this isn't important to me, then what is?"

"How about if we start with a couple of buckets of latex," I suggested. "That'll make a world of difference."

She agreed that would be a good idea, and all our free time was spent painting the house—using a water-based emulsion, since she was pregnant. I assumed that after this exercise she'd forget about the new floor, but it didn't work out that way. Before the last brushstroke had dried, she was off on her bike, checking out all the lumberyards in the immediate vicinity. She returned from a cold, wintry trek to an industrial park on the outskirts of town, and announced that she had bought a new floor. It was a discarded landing stage which had originally been part of the old inner harbor: three hundred and fifty square feet of indestructible teak for eight guilders per linear foot, cut to size.

She'd gone to the local do-it-yourself place and rented some infernal sanding machine, along with a set of rubber kneepads. With her ever-increasing girth, she looked pretty silly inching along, plank by plank, with earplugs in her ears and a dish towel tied around her head. But I had to admit she was right: the floor was beautiful. And she was beautiful, my Raya Mira, as she wiped the sweat from her forehead.

"You just go back to your drawing." She smiled at me over her dust mask. "This is *my* self-portrait."

THERE'S A WHOLE WORLD contained in the face of a child, as if the DNA is already surfacing, unveiling what her destiny is to be. In the conjunction between nose and ears, the outline of the mouth, the arch of the eyebrow and the width of the jaw, we ought to be able to read the future, just as we read the stars by studying the relationship between them. Is she strong? Is she smart? Will she be pretty? Can she sing? Will she suffer the pain of love? Will she stay healthy? I wanted to comprehend the conjunction in which the planets stood on her forehead. Night after night I gazed at the face of my daughter, but the story refused to take shape. I've never been good at reading the stars.

In the end I took heart and turned to my sketchbook and charcoal instead. The first drawing I did was a pile of bedclothes that betrayed the shape of a sleeping child. What is the relation between a model and the maker? Wasn't it a self-portrait in disguise that I was drawing: not the daughter but the father the object of my observations?

I was afraid to throw back the sheet. Like the schoolboy on prom night who secretly watches the girl leaning against the wall, postponing as long as possible the overtures leading to the First Kiss because he isn't sure it will lead to the Kiss.

Not because she's not willing, but because he lacks conviction.

BRECHJE WAS THE ONE who put me on the trail of the search that I hadn't even realized was going on. One winter afternoon she'd taken me out for tea and Beerenburg, while Raya and Lizzy were having a nap. Like Raya, Brechje was a northerner, and she started drinking gin bitters as soon as the sky clouded over and the first trace of night frost appeared on the surface of the water. It was a spontaneous urge, which disappeared again once the ice started to melt.

In our new neighborhood we had discovered a good café, with the unusual name of Cordcheek, where it smelled of cigars and where the aberration of modern café architecture had not yet taken over. Business was slow: the barmaid had turned down the CD—the one hundred best tearjerkers—and was chatting idly with a customer. I was glad that Brechje was there. Jelle had vanished into thin air soon after he met Birgit. I had found it difficult to share fatherhood with my friends. Aside from a sense of pride and the usual anecdotes about how adorable she looked when she did this or that, I could never convey to them the essence of what was going on inside of *me*. I was feeling sorry for myself because it had apparently never occurred to any of them that not only a child had been born, but also a father.

"How's Raya doing?" Brechje asked somewhat superfluously. They talked on the phone every other day.

"You probably know more about that than anyone."

With one finger she was digging little round holes in the pile of the old-fashioned carpet which covered the table. "I mean, how do you think Raya's doing?"

I didn't know what I was supposed to think—I was reminded of Mrs. Ripperda, who was always asking questions like that. I wasn't sure what to say then either. How do I know what I think? Which was probably why she asked the question.

Raya was totally immersed in the care of the infant. The baby had been weaned, but the rest went on as usual: baby food, baby laundry, baby bottles, baby naps. She did everything with great energy and devotion. I'd never suspected there was such an efficient housewife lurking inside my Raya. But I also saw the blissful look on her face when she lay sprawled on the hardwood floor with Lizzy across from her, rolling a ball back and forth, jingling bells, and doing all the other things you do with babies. I envied her the naturalness with which she seemed to do it all.

That's what I told Brechje.

"I guess all of us have some idea of what it is that makes mothers lie on the floor, chirping about bow-wows and moo-cows all day, as if they've suddenly gone soft in the head. We don't hold it against them, not even someone as smart as Raya."

"That's it." I nodded. "She's thrown herself into her new role with heart and soul. Which is good for the baby, good for the emotional bonding, things like that. But I feel like a total imbecile if I spend more than a couple of minutes lying on the floor, fooling around with Lizzy—no matter how dear she is to me. Pretty soon I start thinking: Okay, enough of this; now it's time to do something useful."

"You mean you're not clear about what your relationship to her is?"

"I don't even know if it's about Lizzy. Or about Raya. Women close ranks; I've noticed that. They're all suddenly possessed of this incredibly primitive urge to protect that young life against any possible harm. All those women who crowd around her bed— even you, Brechje!—are totally obsessed by the child. As if the survival of the species is at stake." Now I was the one fiddling with a tuft of the carpet. "Most of the men I know—there aren't all that many—start working like crazy as soon as their first child is born."

"Out slaying dragons, huh?" Brechje said. She smiled as she said it, but I was thinking: Damned if she isn't right. That's what's missing.

"WHEN YOUR MOTHER DIED," she asked me over our second Beerenburg, "did you have that same sense of having been abandoned?"

Ah, my dear mom. How she would have loved to see this grand-child! But she, too, would have joined the women; I was certain of that. She would have bent over the crib with her back to me, like all good fairies.

When she died, I went into deep mourning, but it was a mourn-ing accompanied by great productivity. The death of a mother is so concrete, the pain so recognizable, that it can be shared. And communicated. I told Brechje about the photos I'd taken after reading her written legacy. Not only had I given concrete shape to the pain I felt at her death, I had also found a way to give her life a place of its own. To rescue her life from oblivion.

"You've lost your metaphors," Brechje pronounced.

"What metaphors?" I didn't get the connection.

"A metaphor is nothing but an outflanking movement: you approach the heart of the matter without having to address it in all its rawness. Those photos of your mother are about her and about her life and her belief in what truth is and justice. But most of all, they're about the vulnerability of life itself. The problem with using words like that is that you rob them of their essence. The word trivializes its own meaning. That's why we need metaphors."

"Hey, Brechje's turned philosopher!" There was more irritation in my voice than I intended. "Come on, let's have another one."

I stood up to go over to the bar. She wasn't deterred.

"Listen, Gideon, you're not stupid. In a way, Raya's right when she says that it doesn't get you anywhere, all the hours you spend gazing at Lizzy. It's not about the baby; it's about how you look at her. Not as a father, but as a human being. Forget that you're her father, and look again."

"What would we do without women?" I sighed, and walked away.

"You never give yourself time to really think, Gideon!" she called after me. "You're looking for the solution before you've even figured out what the problem is."

We had another Beerenburg and another—we'd long since forgotten about the tea—and sang along with the one hundred best tearjerkers.

"Shouldn't we be heading home?" I said in her ear, my tongue thick, and she laughed.

"Why? To save Raya?"

We took a long detour along the water, in the direction of her house. I had my arm around her shoulders and there were small clouds of warm air coming out of our mouths. The warmth of Beerenburg and fellowship flowed through my drunken body.

"That's something else men do when they have a baby," she said as we lay in front of her stove with bare feet and hot brandy, "they sleep around, because otherwise they're useless."

"Are they really useless?"

I was struck by my own words. It was the third time I'd asked that same question. Were the other answers so unsatisfactory, or did I just find them hard to accept?

"Well, they're not much use to me, that's for sure." Brechje smiled.

"Don't you want children?" I asked her, and I stroked her belly under her sweater.

"Yeah, sure. A litter of blind witches with red eyes. They'd burn as soon as the sun came up."

"Jesus, Brech, I'm sorry."

It never occurred to me that might be important to her. Her skin really did look as if it had never been touched by the sun.

"Can I see your breasts?"

I took off her sweater and the T-shirt that she wore underneath and fondled her breasts. The hair under her arms was soft and white. I kissed her nipples. They were hard and available to me. My hand went down over her belly, over a cloud of white curly hair, and I felt the steam rise from her body. She opened up to my fingers. My foot curled inside hers, her hand took hold of me, I pulled off my pants, she turned the stove up, I poured brandy in the hollow of her neck, between her breasts, in her navel and farther down, and my tongue followed the rivulet that mingled with her fluid.

I was slaying dragons.

"You won't leave?" Brechje whispered when I entered her.

I thrust once and then pulled back, to watch her desire grow, and her mouth opened and closed like the beak of a bird.

"Yes," I whispered, "before the sun's up."

I knew what I was doing. I wasn't a kid. I was a man.

(IT IS THE PERCEPTION of a face that makes an impression, not the actual image. Something like the difference between a child's portrait by Picasso and one by the school photographer. In the photo only the mother recognizes all the various layers. But what Picasso was painting was not a child—and certainly not one of his own, although they did pose for him—but rather an icon, which over the years becomes crackled. He must have known about the hairline cracks, and the subtle but unmistakable discolorations which would ultimately be its fate. So he anticipated them by painting into the faces of those children the life that awaited them.)

I WAS HOME before the sun came up. I had kissed Brechje and said, "Thank you." She'd smiled and said, "You're welcome." She knew that she had given me a gift, a once-in-a-lifetime, irreplaceable gift. On the way home, I stopped for a cup of coffee at a café where taxi drivers congregate. It was three-thirty in the morning and the glow of the past few hours faded in the merciless fluorescent light that illuminated the Formica tables.

Should I tell Raya about my time with Brechje? Not now, at any rate, I decided. She's too vulnerable, too unstable, too *hormonal*, as she herself used to say. And besides, I didn't think it had anything to do with her. I wrestled with an indivisible question, one that concerned me and me alone. There was no necessity for me to bother her with it, and certainly no need to hurt her.

For the moment I had nothing to say to her.

I wanted to see Lizzy. I did have something to say to her. I had something to offer her.

WHEN I GOT HOME, I went to Lizzy's room and pulled back the sheet that covered her. I clicked a roll of photosensitive film into my camera and placed it on the tripod next to her bed. Gently I took her thumb out of her mouth and laid both her hands on her stomach. Lizzy went on sleeping peacefully. This, I thought, is my daughter. I don't have to make her mine. She *is* mine: my genes, my blood, my thoughts. Here, I thought, is my model. I need no metaphors for her. She is her own metaphor.

In the past few hours I had found myself again, as a man. And gradually it dawned on me that I had become a father. I pushed the button for the first photo. Raya was right: love had to grow under my hands.

THIRTEEN

THE SPEED AT WHICH a life can become transformed is
unbelievable. Human beings are not equipped to keep pace with
it, which is why you're liable to wake up one morning and think to
yourself: Now, where were we?

The overdue maintenance piles up, not only in the laundry
hamper and the drawer with the folders marked *Finances* and *Tax
Returns*, but in your head as well: you can't recall a thought that
struck you last night, something you told yourself you mustn't forget; or suddenly you don't know whether that brilliant idea was
yours or was suggested by someone else. And then you wake up
one morning and you no longer know what your life is all about.

IN A SHORT TIME our house went from well-orchestrated
chaos to total anarchy. This may appear to be a gradual process,
one which you can take your time getting used to, but the opposite is true. You don't get used to it, and what's more, the process
is so insidious that your vigilance is undermined. One day you sit
down in front of the TV with a cup of coffee—tired, tired, tired—
and suddenly you feel something sharp protruding from the seat
of your chair. You lift up the cushion and discover that almost the
entire contents of the kitchen drawer have been deposited there
by your daughter. You look around and suddenly you notice that

everything in the living room is in the wrong place, crooked, torn, full of spots, or in imminent danger of falling over or coming apart.

The little girl is now four years old, but it's as if you've only just gotten over the shock of her arrival. You're still recovering from her birth, so to speak, and there she is standing next to your bed at the crack of dawn, cheerfully requesting toast and marmalade.

That's roughly the relationship between real time and time as you experience it, once you become a parent.

C H I L D H O O D is the ultimate paradox. They say it's the most stressful period in the life of a human being: learning to walk, learning to talk, learning to bond, learning to be good, learning to hold your water—children are deluged with tasks and challenges, all of which are designed to equip them for what we regard as real life. This makes it sound as if the memory of our childhood is like a cartoon in fast-forward: as if that's how fast you're expected to absorb life, to learn how to deal with the new and the strange. But nothing could be farther from the truth. In our memories of childhood, summer is endless and a day at the beach lasts forever. I remember, frame for frame, how we picked red currants in the orchard and slid them from the stem with our fingers, so that the juice ran down our hands and into our sleeves. I remember the sandwiches with sand after a long day at the beach, and how on one occasion that sensation of being suspended in space was rudely disrupted by an incident involving a small dog that had run after a tennis ball thrown too far out into the breakers. I had just learned the word *breakers* and I remember wondering how water could "break," as I stood there in the hot sand, gazing out to sea, where a drama was unfolding.

In our memories those early years lasted so much longer than the years that followed. In childhood we live our lives in slow motion, like the people of the Middle Ages. There's space left over in our young brains, and that space is filled with the time as we live it. Those are *les temps perdus*: back when the hard disk was still empty, recording without complaint or backup the messages it received. We adults consider our lives so very busy and crowded, but of course that's nonsense. Life is becoming more and more routine, as repetition follows upon repetition. It is the hard disk that is glutted. There is less and less space to record impressions; the cells harden into horny tissue.

No wonder so-called young parents always look so jaded. They're expected to empathize with their child, to live life at the same breakneck speed, even though they are no longer equipped for it. They're working with an obsolete system. They're full.

WE WERE DEAD BEAT. I didn't notice at first, just as I didn't notice that there were fewer and fewer utensils in the kitchen drawer. So many things fail to register when life has been reduced to survival—and even that fact escaped me at the time.

I was working for several different magazines, and doing independent work for which there appeared to be a market. Raya had withdrawn to the nest, and from there she ruled over child and house. Once in a while she wrote a piece for her former employer, *Fisheries Bulletin,* but that didn't amount to much. It was because she remained on the sidelines that I was doing well, and this was not lost on me. But she had chosen to stay home with Lizzy: she wanted to experience exactly what it meant to have a child, what it felt like to be a mother. She had a special notebook in which she meticulously recorded her thoughts. It wasn't intended for me, she said, but for Lizzy. For later, when she was older.

Once in a while I saw one of her scribblings, usually no more than half a sheet of paper: a comment on her life, or mine. *Can mothers think?* she asked herself. Or *Are fathers capable of feeling something without dragging themselves into it?*

"Show me your hands," she said once, and a while later there was a scribbled note lying next to the fixative: *What is real work, if the consequences aren't visible?*

SHE HAD DISPENSED with nail polish as soon as the contractions started. In between the pains she busily set about removing the red from her nails, using cotton balls and remover, to the horror of the midwife.

"You've got to stop that! Acetone is very harmful to the fetus."

The midwife made a great show of opening all the windows when she saw that her words were having absolutely no effect on Raya.

"It's not a fetus," Raya retorted, "it's a baby who's going to be born any minute, and it'll scare her out of her wits to be picked up by ten long red fingernails. That's what I call "harmful to the fetus!"

"You should have thought of that before," the midwife said.

Later, when the subject came up again, Raya wanted to know what the midwife could possibly have meant. "I wasn't a mother until then," she spluttered. "How could I have thought of it before?"

Raya demonstrated great foresight in deciding to file her nails: there is nothing quite so fragile as the skin of a newborn baby. A wedding band is enough to produce a scratch, and pressing too hard when you fasten the diaper can result in a bruise on the hipbone. Raya was mortally afraid of hurting her child in any way, and she kept her nails short, even when it was no longer necessary.

"When are you going to let them grow again?" I asked her. Lizzy was well past the newborn stage and had started accumulating her own scratches and bruises.

"When I'm an ex-mother," was the cryptic reply.

"In other words, never, my dear Raya!" I found her naivete touching. "There are some things in life that never go away. Motherhood is a chronic condition."

"Do you really think so, Gideon?" She looked at me as if I had just come up with a totally new insight. "Of course, I know that's what they say, the model mothers, and of course they write things like that in *Libelle* and all . . . But can it possibly be true that you'll never ever be alone with yourself again?"

That evening she bent over her notebook with an intensity I had not seen for a long time. I was under the impression that Raya lived in perfect harmony with the choices she had made; that she found fulfillment in her life with Lizzy, in the minute observations of that life, as it grew under her hands; that she was not afraid of the staggering love she felt for her child.

That night, before she went to bed, there was a note for me: *Will there never again be a day that I can think my own thoughts, cherish my own feelings, pursue my own dreams, rule over my own body, without another voice inside me? Will there never again be a day when I coincide with myself, with no one else in between?*

IT WAS THAT MORNING, the morning after she wrote that note, that I suddenly realized how totally enervated we were. For whatever reason—perhaps because of the note, or the grimness with which it was written—I had slept badly and woke up exhausted. I was relieved that—as always—Raya had taken care of the daily preliminaries: the coffee was in the thermos jug, Lizzy was sitting contentedly at the table, experimenting with paint and segments of orange, the curtains were open, and sunlight gleamed on the hardwood floor, which had increasingly inclined toward green since it had been installed in our living room.

Raya was out on the deck with a mug of coffee. There were pouches under her eyes, I even thought I detected a touch of dandruff in her hair, and her skin was ashen in the pale morning light. I looked at the hands that held the coffee mug, the hands I had fallen in love with. They had lost none of their strength but they were older, more worn. Although she did all the housework herself— she refused to take on a cleaning woman because she was convinced that it was good for children to see their parents actually working—at that moment they were lying idle in her lap. As if she had no idea what to do with the strength they harbored.

"I think I've lost my way," I heard her say from behind her mug. She turned to look at me and burst out laughing. "Do you have any idea how you look?"

"Lost my way, too?" I grinned.

"Not to mention a good bit of your hair."

"What would you say to a break?"

It had been too long since we'd been anywhere. The absence of devoted grandparents had increasingly made itself felt.

"I want to go to sea again," she said. "My hands are getting stiff."

Every once in a while the bug bit: seasickness. It wasn't the first time that I'd seen it happen, although now she seemed to be in earnest. She hadn't been on any long trips since we met. The last one was five years ago: a clipper on the Baltic Sea. Since then she'd settled for short trips, usually charters, lasting only a week or two. She returned with matted hair and callused hands and then wrote magnificent short stories for obscure literary journals. And sometimes not even that. And after a while she dried up again.

"I think I'll give them a call," Raya said.

I knew that *them* referred to her friends at *Fisheries Bulletin*. That meant it wouldn't be a charter this time.

"Then I guess I'd better start making plans," I replied.

THE SKIPPER turned out to be Jo den Heyer, a former fisherman who looked like he had a long-standing acquaintance with the bottle; the mate on board was his nephew Jo den Heyer, skinny, pockmarked, and shy as a ship's cat. Old Jo had sold his clipper for good money to a dentist with a sense of adventure and was now employed by the Toxopeus shipyards. I was aware of the firm's reputation: they built luxury yachts for the kind of millionaire who lives in Monaco and parks his capital in the Cape Verde Islands. It was Jo's job to deliver these floating palaces to the specified destination, and on the way to test the rigging and equipment. This time it was a two-master with electric reefing apparatus, GPS, and automatic twin foresail. None of that meant anything to me, but Raya was over the moon. She'd never sailed in such luxury before. When I ventured to inquire if calluses and inspiration might not fall victim to such opulence, she shook her head vehemently: with an alcoholic at the helm and an overgrown adolescent as mate, there was plenty of hard work waiting for her. Above and below deck.

AT FOUR O'CLOCK in the morning I started our old Volkswagen diesel and kept the motor running until it had warmed up. Then I bundled Lizzy into a blanket and settled her on the backseat. The early morning displayed the first signs of fall, there was a lot of moisture in the air, and the cobwebs in the ivy sparkled in the headlight beams. Raya threw her duffel bag into the back and seated herself next to me, a thermos of coffee between her legs. She'd been awake for hours, and the adrenaline was coursing through her body. As the car made its way through the sleeping landscape, she stared into the darkness, wide-eyed and silent, as if she were already standing on the forward deck, searching for the beacon that would determine her course.

In the first rays of the sun, with Lizzy half-asleep in my arms, I watched as my wife stepped on board the *Schöne Erna*, a gleaming monster which in the bleak morning light looked even more imposing than it was. Time was getting short and the greetings she exchanged with Jo and Jo were brief. The old guy was anxious to get Rotterdam behind him, since he had a horror of the tankers under Maltese flag that steamed mercilessly up toward the New Waterway. In the pilothouse Raya was quickly briefed. Then she stepped back onto the quay to cast off. The doors of the lock gates were open, and in the distance rose a landscape which was a strange mixture of land and water. As if we'd been given a short reprieve before our separation became a fact. The open sea concealed itself from our gaze.

It was not until that moment—or so it seemed to me—when she stepped from the rail onto the quay to cast off, that she realized that I was standing there: her husband, with her child in his arms. The feverish eyes of the past few hours focused again. The look she gave me was questioning, searching. As we embraced, Lizzy woke up and began crying as if her heart would break. A shout from the captain sounded from close by and I could hear the water swirling out from underneath the hull. Young Jo stood on the forward deck, looking impatiently back and forth between the wooden gates of the lock and the little scene on the quay.

"What are your plans?" she asked at the last minute.

"How long will you be gone?"

"Jo!" She turned to look back in the direction of the pilothouse. "How long will we be gone?"

"I don't have a clue," he boomed. "Do you?"

I WATCHED from the dike as the ship passed through the lock gates fifteen or twenty feet below. Raya stood on the afterdeck, the faraway look back in her eyes, hands held tensely at her sides. A clipper barge entered the lock a short distance from the *Schöne Erna*. The lockmaster gestured.

"Third bollard!" Jo shouted.

Young Jo stood nervously at the rail, ready with the enormous fenders. Raya grabbed the hawser and slung it around the third bollard. With her full weight she braked the ship. She waved to us; we waved back. The gates closed; the locking could begin.

A FEW HOURS LATER I lay on our former landing stage and looked into the green eyes of my daughter.

"Well, Lizzy, what are we going to do?"

The leave-taking had been difficult and the flood of tears al-most impossible to check, but now, as we lay side by side in the morning sun amid the litter of a hasty departure, she'd gradually become calmer.

"Do!" she trumpeted.

Do—it sounded like a good idea to me. But what?

FOURTEEN

GREEN EYES, I know that for certain. As green as the sea on an autumn afternoon. As green as the sky just before a thunderstorm. As green as the floor in our house.

Three feet, five and a quarter inches. I know that for certain, too. We never stood her against the doorpost and drew a pencil mark level with her head, like everyone else does. That's why I don't know how tall she was when she was two, or five. Only when she was four. Just over four.

One foot was larger than the other, that's something else I'm sure of. The difference was only about a fifth of an inch, but that's a lot when the feet are so small. I don't know how big her feet were, maybe four inches, or eight. I also don't remember whether both feet ended up being the same size, whether the smaller foot grew faster during the last year of her life.

Some things I just don't remember.

Orange was her favorite color. Orange complements green, maybe that's why. Maybe I once said something like: "Orange looks nice on you, with your green eyes," and that's how it became her favorite color.

That's the way kids are, I know: they like nothing better than to please their parents.

I'D FOUND SOME ROLLS of wallpaper up in the attic.
Raya and I had once planned to paper the hall, but we never got
around to it. Now I took the rolls downstairs and spread the paper
out across the floor. Three long strips next to each other, fastened
in the corners with thumbtacks. We had to climb over the couch
to get to the kitchen—but we didn't mind.

"Lie down," I said to Lizzy, who was standing naked in the middle of the room.

We'd bought lots and lots of poster paint and fat brushes made
of hog's bristles. We'd turned the stove up high: it was a dreary fall
day, one of those days when it's almost impossible to drive the
cold out of your bones. We'd made ourselves a pan of hot chocolate, which was now standing on the stove in the living room.

Lizzy had woken up crying that morning. Raya had been away
at sea for over a month, and she hadn't cried for her mother since
the deluge of tears on the way home. We were getting along fine,
just the two of us.

In the morning I'd take Lizzy to school and then work my tail
off all day, so that at five o'clock I could pick her up at a girlfriend's
house, do the shopping, cook dinner, watch *Sesame Street*, and get her
into her nightgown. This was followed by the brushing of teeth,
the bedtime story, the rearrangement of stuffed animals, a good-
night kiss, a song, the door ajar, and one last kiss—after which I
spent the whole evening in the darkroom, finishing whatever I hadn't
gotten around to during the day. Sometimes I forgot to make her a
sandwich to take to school. Her hair didn't look as neat as usual
(only women have the knack of taming springy hair, and I could
always tell by looking at the hairdos of Lizzy's classmates which of
the parents had gotten the children ready for school that morning). Sometimes I forgot to brush her teeth or give her vitamin
pills. And it was my fault that she appeared one morning dressed
as a fairy, because I thought that it was her teacher's birthday and
all the kids were allowed to dress up. We were a week early.

But outside of that, we were getting along just fine.

"Never mind," Lizzy said bravely, when she was the only fairy in the schoolyard. I'd taught her that. I told her it helps when, just for a minute, you're not quite sure what to do.

BUT ON THIS particular morning even that didn't help. She'd woken up screaming and was now ensconced under the covers. She cried so hard that it made me angry.

"Then talk to me, Lizzy!" I shouted.

The seven stuffed animals had been thrown all over the room. She buried her face in the pillow. She turned her back on me, kicked, wound herself in the bedclothes. And cried and screamed. In the end I left her alone in her room. I resisted the urge to slam the door behind me. Luckily I saw the sneaker just in time and gently wedged it between the frame and the door, to keep it ajar.

I called the school: "Lizzy isn't feeling well today. I'm going to keep her home."

Her teacher was very understanding.

Then I called the lab, where they'd had to work overtime because I needed my negatives by nine o'clock this morning. "I'll pick them up tomorrow. My daughter isn't feeling well today." I sensed a bit less understanding there.

Then I called my client. At which point I began to understand why some mothers reach for the sherry at ten in the morning.

In the backyard I took a deep breath. I was angry with Lizzy because she couldn't control her grief. I was angry with Raya. I was very, very angry with Raya. How could she do it? Desert your child, just like that, and your husband—who also happened to be the wage earner in the family, I thought, with growing indignation. Because your "hands are getting stiff." What utter nonsense! In the meantime I'd missed out on thousands of guilders' worth of work because her absence forced me to limit the number of jobs I took on. (The money wasn't actually a problem, since Raya and I had agreed on how far we could afford to eat into our savings. But of course that didn't count now.)

It was irresponsible, going off like that, without giving me any idea when she'd be back. That's what it was: irresponsible. Her daughter was falling apart. And I was the one who had to pick up the pieces.

"Daddy, shall I go to school after all?"

Lizzy was standing next to me, her face still red and swollen from crying. She'd dressed herself. She was wearing a pair of tights (backward) and a summer sweater that was too small for her. She'd put on her rubber boots—she didn't know how to tie her shoelaces yet. And she'd tried to brush her hair.

"You're not going anywhere, sweetie. Today we're staying home."

I faked a bout of sneezing and ran to the john to blow my nose.

THE DAY BEFORE, a letter had arrived from Raya, who now had firm ground under her feet on some exotic island and gave us an account of her travels. Of course, she'd called from time to time via Satcom, but this letter was different: she had stories to tell.

That's why it was my fault: I should have known better. But in the euphoria of the moment I forgot that it was always wise to exercise some degree of censorship when it came to Raya's writings— even in the case of her daughter. She'd written a fairy tale for Lizzy, which I read to her before she went to sleep that night. The consequences of the story, as I would learn later, were inevitable.

I should have known better.

Dear Lizzy,

I'm sitting on the roof of a house and looking out over the sea. We got to the island where we're delivering the boat in the early evening. It's nighttime now, and above my head there are thousands of stars. You see lots more stars here than at home, because it's so dark. That means that even the smallest star, with only a bit of light, is strong enough to be seen.

Sometimes a star falls to earth, and then I make a wish.

Someday I'll take you with me, so you can see all these stars for yourself. Then you can make a wish when one of them falls. What would you wish for, Lizzy?

I don't know when I'll be coming back. Daddy says that you're doing fine, the two of you, and I'm sure he's right. I miss you both and once in a while that makes me sad, but sometimes I see things or I come to a new place and I think, One day you'll see all this too, I'm sure of it. That makes me feel a little better.

Somewhere along the way—in the Arctic, way up north, where the wind blows hailstones and you can skate on the ocean—a long dike came into sight, covered with grass and dotted with flowers in all different colors. On the dike, quite far apart, there were apple trees in bloom. It was raining pink petals. It was all so beautiful, so cheery and colorful that it looked like a painting.

I asked the captain of the ship why there was a dike here and why everything was in flower in the middle of winter. He told me that long, long ago, during the coldest winter anyone could remember, the ice at the North Pole started to break up, and that the ice floes slid right over the dike and came to rest against a little house where two sisters lived. Their names were Suzie and Rosa. They lived together in the house at the foot of the dike; it was painted white and had sky-blue shutters.

The two sisters were just as pretty as you, with long black hair and green eyes. They looked exactly alike, and yet they were very different. Suzie's skin was as pale as a lily because she'd never seen the sun, and Rosa's skin was soft and pink from the open air. Rosa liked to stand on the dike and look out to sea. Suzie preferred to sit indoors, where she made paintings of what she thought she'd see if she went outside.

"Rosa, you're going to catch cold!" said Suzie, and she knitted a warm scarf for her sister.

"Suzie, you have no idea how beautiful the world is!" said Rosa, and she told her sister all about the sea and the boats that she saw gliding past.

One day Rosa came back from a walk along the dike. It was windy out and there were tears running down her cheeks. Suzie took a warm towel and dried Rosa's face. But the tears went on running down Rosa's cheeks.

"What's wrong, my dear little sister?" Suzie asked, suddenly frightened.

"Oh, Suzie, it hurts so much to tell you! But I have to leave you. I have to find out what's on the other side of the water and beyond the horizon."

The girls cried all night, and when the sun came up they fell asleep in each other's arms.

The next morning Suzie carefully packed Rosa's suitcase. She put in all the warm woolen socks and sweaters she'd ever knitted. And at the bottom of the suitcase she put in her most beautiful painting. Then Rosa boarded a large sailing ship with three masts. As the ship sailed away, she climbed up into the tallest mast so that she could see across the dike to where Suzie was looking out the window and waving to her.

Weeks went by. Every morning Suzie stood at the window to see if she could see if her sister was coming over the dike. But Rosa didn't come back. The little house was getting more and more crowded, since Suzie had started painting all the countries, all the skies, and all the trees and birds and plants that she thought Rosa might see on her travels. Every morning she stood by the window, ready to show Rosa her paintings and to ask her, "Is this how it was, Rosa? Have we both really seen exactly the same things?"

But Rosa didn't come back.

The weeks turned into months and the months into years. Suzie had already circled the earth three times in her head. She had seen the

North Pole and the South Pole; she had walked through jungles and climbed snow-covered mountaintops. She had sailed the high seas for days without ever catching a glimpse of land. She never knew that the sea could take on so many different faces. The little house at the bottom of the dike was so full of paintings that there was only room for a bed and the easel. All the wood in the house had been sawed into pieces to frame the paintings, even the legs of her bed.

When all the wood inside the house had been used up, Suzie dressed warmly and went outside for the very first time in her life. It was a lovely morning in spring, the apple tree in the garden was in flower, and the birds were singing their songs. Suzie was carrying her basket with knitting yarn, and as she walked by she picked up the branches the apple tree had lost during the winter. When she got to the top of the dike, she planted the branches in the ground; then she took her knitting yarn and put up a washing line that was many miles long. She went on walking until her yarn was all gone; she went all the way to the end of the dike.

After that she went on painting, but now she no longer peered out the window to see if her sister was coming. No, after that she climbed up onto the dike every morning and hung the paintings she had done the previous night on the line to dry.

One night Suzie saw her sister in a dream: the big three-master ship on which Rosa had sailed away had been lost in a raging storm. Suzie saw the ship slowly sinking into an inky-black sea full of icebergs and ice floes. Rosa was sitting in the crow's nest and waving to her as the ship sank slowly—very slowly—beneath the waves.

The next night Rosa again appeared to her in a dream. She was lying under the ice, facing upward, and Suzie saw her as if she were looking through a misty windowpane. Her long black hair floated around her head like seaweed. "Come!" Rosa beckoned. "Come." Her mouth moved, but there was no sound to be heard.

Night after night the dreams recurred, and feverishly Suzie painted all these visions from the depths of the frozen sea, under the polar cap—for that was where her sister was; she was sure of it. When all the paint and all the canvas had been used up, winter came again and the ice at the North Pole began to break up. Enormous ice floes floated southward, defied the lukewarm seas, and crept up the side of the dike. They came up so high that one day Suzie looked out the window and saw that her house was buried under the ice. She wrapped a woolen scarf around her head, took the latest painting under her arm, and opened the door of her little house.

"I'm coming," she called to Rosa, and from far away she heard, "Come!"

"I'm coming," Suzie called, and again came the echo of Rosa's voice: "Come!"

When that terrible winter came to an end and the thaw set in, the people of this country found two dead girls buried in the ice. They both had long black hair and were wearing the same warm woolen scarf. But what they found even more surprising was the fact that each of them had a painting clutched in her arms: one was framed; the other was only canvas. When they took the paintings carefully from the girls' arms, they saw that the water and ice had erased the colors. The canvases were blank. The paintings which were so precious to the two girls will forever remain a secret.

THE BOOTS had been kicked off; the tears had been dried. Lizzy was now sitting on my lap, bundled up in a blanket and licking a large pink lollipop. I considered this an excellent breakfast for a little girl who had slept badly and woken up in tears. We were sitting on the deck under the eaves, watching how the clouds gathered, blotting out the last traces of blue.

"Do you miss Mommy?" I had no idea how to broach the subject without precipitating another flood of tears.

There was no answer for a long time.

"Do you?" I tried again.

"You never make fish sticks," came the peevish reply from the depths of the blanket.

"I hate fish sticks. That's why."

"Well, I don't."

Again it was still for a while.

"And outside of that?"

"Is Mommy coming back?"

"Of course she is, sweetie."

(WHAT I WANTED to say was, You can never be sure, Lizzy, just like you can never be sure when she goes out shopping. Or when the baby-sitter comes and we go off to see a play. That's one of the things that makes life so unbearable, Lizzy, the fact that you never know whether everything is going to stay the same. Whether there'll be a new day tomorrow. And whether that day will be like today, as you hope it will. But that's not what I said.

And I didn't say, I don't know whether Raya will be coming back. I didn't say, I'm not sure, because I don't know your mother well enough to be confident that she'll come back.

What I said was what she wanted to hear. What I had to say. What I wanted to hear.)

"SHALL WE PAINT HER?"

"Paint Mommy?"

"Yes. And then we'll hang her on the wall."

"One for in the living room and one for in the kitchen?"

"Why not?"

"And one for you to take to bed with you?"

I went up to the attic and brought down the rolls of wallpaper. We pinned three six-foot strips to the green floor with thumb-tacks. They stretched from one wall to the other. Then we hopped on the bike and went to Hema to buy poster paint.

"You first!" she said.

"You first!" I said.

Then she took off her clothes.

"Lie down," I said, and she lay down on the middle strip of paper. With broad strokes of black, I painted the outline of my daughter. She had a cowlick right in the middle of her crown. Her shoulders were narrow. I noticed how thin she was. I discovered a birthmark on her forearm. One foot was larger than the other.

"How tall are you, Lizzy?"

"Three," she answered firmly. "For sure."

"Three what?" I asked.

"Three tall, of course, silly!"

I went and got the yardstick: three feet, three and a quarter inches.

"You were right. In fact, you're over three feet tall."

After I'd finished painting around her, she put on her bathrobe. Then I took off my clothes and lay down on the strip of wallpaper closest to the window. If she spills paint, at least it won't be on the couch, I thought. Lizzy dipped the brush into the can of red paint.

"For Christ's sake, Lizzy, be careful." A big blob of paint had landed in my hair.

"I'm sorry," came the murmured reply.

Jerk, I thought to myself.

Later we dissolved into helpless laughter and she painted my legs blue.

"What about Mommy?"

We stood on the couch to admire the results. Lizzy was green with lots of orange. I was monochromatic red, no nose and no eyes. All around us were hundreds of footprints: big red footprint, small yellow footprint, big brown footprint, small white footprint. Thousands of toes formed the foliage of an impressionistic autumn forest above our heads.

With our feet in the paint tray we drank lukewarm chocolate with a skin on top. We showered and a penitent Lizzy scrubbed the blue paint off my legs with a sisal mitt. Then we climbed back onto the couch and looked at the third strip: except for a few stray drops of paint, it was blank.

"Shall I draw a mommy?" I suggested, but she rejected that idea.

So we went upstairs and got Raya's old jeans, a ratty-looking T-shirt she couldn't bear to throw out, and a pair of heavy woolen socks. My resentment had not yet subsided. I rummaged around in the shed and came back with a jar of epoxy glue. I glued Raya's clothes to the wallpaper. Then I dipped the brush in purple paint and drew a circle for the head.

"Now it's your turn, Lizzy!" I cheered her on.

She dipped her feet in the paint and marched murderously over her mother.

FIFTEEN

THE DAYS that I felt like a complete idiot every time I squatted down so that I was on a level with Lizzy lay far behind me. Without a trace of embarrassment I helped her do a wee-wee behind the playground teeter-totter, and there was a definite flair to the way I squeezed through the automatic doors of the bus with child and stroller. Doing the Bert and Ernie jigsaw puzzle together was no longer a waste of time: it was a fact of life.

It wasn't habituation. There are some things you never get used to. You can't say, Now I'm used to my father or mother, or, Slowly but surely I'm getting used to myself. Habituation has to do with something outside yourself. You can get used to a new house, or an irritating habit your sister-in-law has, even a leaky faucet. But you can't become accustomed to something that is inextricably linked to yourself. You don't get used to a clubfoot: you either have it or you don't, and all you can do is accept it.

It's the same with a child: by the time you've become really close, there's nothing left to get used to, only things to reconcile. For Raya Mira that process began with the conception; her fusion with that new life kept pace with the growth of the child, and after that the reconciliation began. After the birth of Lizzy, Raya had to get used to the demands that this new life placed on her, but the child herself, the existence of that child, was as natural as the scar between her shoulder blades.

But as a father, how do you fuse with something that didn't grow out of you? How do you reconcile yourself with a meteorite that lands on your roof? The impossibility of that challenge is terrifying. I understand why men jump into bed with the next-door neighbor during the pregnancy of their beloved; I understand the workaholics and the temporary alcoholics. Nature has given us—fathers—no handhold, no way of catching the meteorite before being crushed by it: suddenly, from one day to the next, you have a Child, you're a Father, and in keeping with the standards and expectations of the day, you're expected to Make Something of It.

There's no time for fusion—so either you run away or you resign yourself to waiting for the moment of reconciliation.

M Y   R E C O N C I L I A T I O N began the day that the thrashing chicken had its neck well and truly wrung: Raya Mira was on the *Schöne Erna* and it was sink or swim. I decided to swim—and to do it with a song. For me, having total responsibility for the well-being of my daughter opened the way to my fatherhood.

I'd found my handhold.

L I Z Z Y   A N D   I had gotten into the habit of feeding the ducks on Saturday morning. There's nothing spectacular about that— half the families in the country feed the ducks on weekends—but in our little household it developed into a veritable ritual.

At the breakfast table we discussed the matter of exactly how much bread was good for the ducks (in other words, how many crusts Lizzy was allowed to leave on her plate). Later the relative merits of white and whole wheat became a topic of conversation (whole wheat is better for ducks, she decided). And then we were confronted with the problem of how to see to it that all the ducks in the pond got their share, and how to prevent that one macho male from stealing bread away from the shy one.

After a couple of weeks of duck feeding, Lizzy became troubled by the thought that although we fed the ducks in the pond near our house, the other ducks in town didn't get one crumb of our bread.

"But wait a minute, sweetie," I protested. (I could see myself pedaling off on some tomfool tour of all the ponds in the city because my daughter was developing a sense of social justice.) "Don't you think that there are kids who take their old bread to the ducks in all the other ponds?"

"How do you know?" she snapped.

"I don't know for sure, but that's what I think. It's only logical."

"Well, I don't think so." That appeared to be the end of the discussion.

I tried a different approach: "But suppose, just suppose, that there are boys and girls standing there at the edge of the pond and that those boys and girls want to take care of their ducks all by themselves. . . . They wouldn't like it very much if you came along and tried to feed their ducks."

"You can't know whether there are other kids standing there, Daddy!"

She pushed back her chair with an angry shove and went to stand sullenly at the kitchen counter.

"Okay, okay." Lizzy knew that I couldn't stand it when she turned her back on me. "We'll see."

I took the street map of the city from the kitchen drawer and spread it out on the table.

"Look, this is our pond." I pointed to a spot on the map. Lizzy went into the living room and came back with her box of felt-tipped pens. With a blue pen she circled the dot that represented our pond.

"Okay, what now?" I asked, and pointed out the other ponds on the map.

Lizzy chose one of the other dots. It was in another part of town and we mapped out a route that would take us to our new destination.

Gradually her concern for the well-being of the ducks was transferred to the play of lines and circles on the map, which now occupied a prominent place on the wall above the kitchen table. Like true warlords, we pinned little flags to the ponds that we had already visited, and colored in the routes we had taken with a red pen. We discussed the strategy we would follow to get to the next destination; it was a challenge never to use the same route twice. In the end the ducks were only a flimsy excuse to cycle around the city in search of new routes. Sometimes we even forgot the bread.

Until suddenly the country was in the grip of a freeze.

"DADDY!" Lizzy was standing next to my bed, blind panic in her eyes. I sat up with a start. It wasn't quite seven o'clock in the morning.

"What's the matter?"

"Daddy! It's freezing outside. There's ice everywhere. Look!"

To convince me, she pulled open the bedroom curtain. Against the background of a pitch-black sky, I saw the ice flowers on the windowpane. Lizzy was close to tears, and it took an effort not to smile at her distress.

"But sweetie, ice flowers are beautiful!"

"The ducks"—and now she was crying—"they'll all freeze to death. We have to go look!" And impatiently she pulled at my sleeve.

I decided to play along, and hurriedly we got dressed. Checking the map quickly, we decided which route we'd take, and jumped on the bike to take stock of the damage. The city was the very picture of calm—Lizzy was a real morning person, like her mother—and we biked through a winter landscape that was virtually untouched. White frost draped the trees like angel hair, and there was a layer of ice on the water—that was all.

It was by no means a severe frost.

Lizzy heaved a sigh of relief: the ducks walked flat-footed across the barely frozen water with a cheerful air, pecking at the odd blade of grass protruding from the mud. Her fears had been premature.

THE SUDDEN ARRIVAL of winter lent an extra dimension to our campaign. Armed not only with the usual bread crusts, but also a stick and a spade, we set off to rescue the duck population from certain death. Blue flags appeared on our map to mark the ponds that froze over quickly; green flags signified the ponds which were apparently fed by a discharge of warm water and had no need of our help.

Lizzy proved to be a conscientious administrator—like her father.

And for this reason it was strange that on one of our tours we discovered a small pond that had escaped her attention. It was in the middle of a neglected public garden on the edge of a run-down neighborhood, where the local shopkeepers had been bought out by chain stores like Blockbuster and Carpetland, and the occupants concealed themselves behind lace curtains. I didn't recognize the spot and, even relying on my mental map, I couldn't say for sure whether the park had always been there. But that appeared to be the case. An old weeping willow hung over the pond, its branches rotting in the frozen water—it had certainly not been planted yesterday—and apparently there had once been a wooden bridge over the narrow part of the pond. The foundations were still intact.

Lizzy dutifully trudged all around the pond and reported her findings: yes, she'd found quite a few ducks under the trees, and no, they didn't seem to have any extra fat on them. She took the bread crusts out of the saddlebags, along with a spade. I left her to it.

Because the leaves had fallen, I could look through the bare branches of the trees to the row of houses that bordered the park:

imposing nineteenth-century villas with their back to this dilapi-
dated neighborhood. Now I suddenly caught on to the logic of
what I had taken to be a public park. It had never been intended
as such: these were the former gardens of one of those villas. Two
brick pillars, covered in moss, caught my eye.

On one it said *Little* and on the other *Heaven*.

"Liz," I called to Lizzy, who was standing under the weeping
willow, "I'm going over to those houses for a minute."

I pointed in the direction of the villas and she gestured that
she'd understood.

AT THE CORNER of the park I checked the street sign on
one of the houses: *Wenckebachlaan*. I was on the right track.
Through the bare winter gardens I saw my daughter pottering
around with the ducks and her bag of bread. There was still not a
soul to be seen. It was early morning, of course, but I couldn't remember any other trek having led us to a spot as deserted as this.
It didn't appear to bother Lizzy.

Little Heaven had the air of a haunted house that had long
since been deserted. The paint was peeling and the lawn was so
overgrown with dead lupines and knee-high nettles that it resembled a neglected botanical garden. All it needed was a few shutters
banging in the wind and a front door hanging off its hinges to
complete the cliché of the tumbledown villa.

In the front yard there was a faded real estate sign which, to my
joy, bore a sticker reading *Sold*. My relief was entirely sentimental:
it was in this house that I had met Raya Mira. I couldn't bear the
thought of Little Heaven being demolished. It was bad enough
contemplating the sight of it now, unloved and abandoned.

A LARGE CAR STOPPED in the driveway. I automatically
turned around to check that the small figure in the purple coat was
still within my range of vision. Lizzy was standing next to the remains
of the wooden bridge, making holes in the ice with her spade.

The car door swung open and there stood Jelle on the sidewalk, with a broad grin on his face.

"Just bought it!" he shouted, radiating pride.

"What? You?" I shouted back, astonishment written all over me.

It was a remarkable opening dialogue. Jelle and I hadn't seen each other in over two years, and during that time we had seldom talked on the phone, actually not since his marriage to Birgit Bijvoet, although that was hardly her fault. Birgit and Jelle proved to bring out the best in each other, career-wise. She had quit her job as nutritional consultant to a multinational firm and, with considerable business insight, had set up her own line of organic products for children. Her business was booming. Moreover, within a few short years Jelle had become one of the most sought-after commercial photographers of the day, thanks mainly to his mother's Rolodex (although he'd bite off his tongue before admitting it), which made him unapproachable for the likes of me. If he wasn't in Milan, then it was Tahiti or some other Olympian peak.

And now he was standing here on the Wenckebachlaan in front of Little Heaven, which he had apparently purchased.

"For Pete's sake, Jelle," I said, after an elaborate greeting, "I knew that you and Birgit weren't short of cash, but how on earth can you afford it? It'll cost hundreds of thousands of guilders to get a ruin like this whipped into shape."

"Dad died." He grinned.

"And you didn't think to tell me?"

I hadn't realized that we'd drifted so far apart that he'd neglected to notify me of his father's death.

"Don't worry about it. My mother turned the cremation into one of the social events of the season: caterers, tents all over the lawn, string quartet on the patio—you get the idea. Just one big festival of self-gratification. You didn't miss anything."

Just maybe, I thought, I might have wanted to come (and I added *bastard*). It wouldn't have done me any harm to hobnob with the contents of Mrs. Ripperda's address book. But I didn't say so. That would have sounded too envious.

"Are you two expecting?" I asked, with a nod in the direction of the house. I'd already noticed he was driving one of those SUVs built for six kids, where the backseat is usually occupied by one spoiled brat and a Labrador.

"On the contrary. We've decided against having children."

"Who writes your copy, Jelle? As if you've just decided to take the green couch instead of the red one. Have you even tried? Or can't you have kids?" I ended cautiously.

"Gideon, we don't *want* children." Curtness. Annoyance. Alienation.

As we talked, we strolled around the house. Here and there Jelle poked a yardstick into the rotten window frames. It was as if he were talking to me on his cell phone: the lukewarm interest that tells you someone's doing God-knows-what while you're trying hard to keep a flagging conversation going.

"Having children isn't something you just suddenly decide against," I joked.

"Gideon, why should people be free to just decide they *do* want something but not to just decide they *don't* want something? We aren't interested in having kids."

(Wasn't it Socrates who said, "Whoever doesn't think that there's something he lacks doesn't long for what he doesn't think he lacks"?)

I searched for words to rectify the awkward turn the conversation was taking.

"I guess I understand how you feel, Jelle. Sometimes I can think of a lot of things that are more fun than kids. Anyway, I'd better go check on Lizzy. She's over there by the pond. She was worried about the ducks. Want to come along?"

JELLE CAME ALONG. As he described at some length how they were planning to renovate the house, and told me about the interior decorator Birgit had found who—interestingly enough—turned out to be an artist, I was the one who'd switched to cell-phone mode.

I wondered whether their childlessness had to do with the death of his father. Not that Jelle had ever struck me as someone who was crazy about kids...but neither would I have expected him to deliberately opt for a life without children. Maybe Birgit had some terrible experience as a child and Jelle's love for her was stronger than his desire to have children—who knows?

But his words echoed in my head: why wasn't it possible to just not want something? There was some truth in this. When two people don't have children, everyone secretly speculates about the real reason behind their choice—if it is a choice. No one ever wonders why the rest of the world does choose to have children. Are we so collectively programmed that procreation is the rule, always and everywhere, and declining to have children the exception? And why is there this need to clarify, explain, even justify that exception?

Perhaps the need to provide an explanation stems from envy. We are envious of someone who opts for himself, rather than being guided by a biological urge to procreate. It's the conflict between self-preservation and the preservation of the species—between the individual and the collective good.

That's enough to turn anyone green with envy.

"Is that Lizzy?" I heard Jelle's voice next to me. Apparently he had concluded his exposition on finance schemes and the fiscal advantages which the villa represented. We were standing on the edge of the pond and my thoughts were elsewhere. "I wouldn't have recognized her in a month of Sundays."

"Yeah, she's gotten so big." I mumbled the obligatory reply and looked around absently for the purple coat.

Damn it! Lizzy!

(How long had I been gone? Ten minutes, a quarter of an hour maybe. What made me think that a four-year-old was capable of taking care of herself? Why is there no one around in this godforsaken place? Why didn't I stay with her? How many days has the temperature been below zero? How strong is the ice?)

"Lizzy, come here! This minute! No, wait, stay where you are. I'll come to you."

There she was: standing in the middle of the frozen pond behind Little Heaven with a plastic bag full of crusts in one hand and her spade in the other. At first it was as if what I was saying didn't register with her. She just stood there, looking slightly dazed, with the ducks all around her, and then started inching farther out onto the ice.

"Lizzy, stop! I'm coming!"

"Don't be stupid," Jelle muttered next to me; "you'd go straight through the ice."

He reached into his pocket for his cell phone.

"Thirty-five pounds, is she over thirty-five pounds, Gideon?" he shouted a little later. I was on the other side of the pond, desperately searching for a long branch, a piece of rope, a ladder.

"How should I know?" I shouted back. "Why?"

"The fire department. They say the ice is strong enough to hold thirty-five pounds."

"Tell them she weighs fifty pounds, or seventy-five!" I shouted, the panic rising. "They've got to come; the ice is breaking around her."

The ice was breaking around her.

In the deadly silence of the next few seconds all I heard was the underwater reverberation of soft, breaking ice. *Ping. Ping. Ping.* Jelle was standing on the opposite side of the pond, pressing the telephone to his ear with one hand and gesturing violently with the other. In the middle stood a little girl, no longer of this world, wearing a purple coat and carrying a plastic bag and a spade.

"Lizzy, can you hear me?" I shouted, my hands cupped around my mouth.

She looked up, but did not reply. She was standing still now. Did she know the danger she was in?

"Lizzy, listen to me!" I tried to hold her attention. I thought, If only she stays where she is, if only she doesn't start walking. God, let her feet freeze to the spot until the fire department gets here.

"Liz, sweetie! The fire department is on the way. They'll get you off the ice. Nothing's going to happen. Stay where you are. Everything's okay! Just stay there! I'm not angry! Stay there, Lizzy! I love you! Stay there ... stay ... stay ..."

In the distance I heard the sirens getting closer. Jelle took up his position at the entrance to the park. Lizzy stood on the ice—in the middle of an ever-widening star, with more and more black lines leading from the center to the edge. *Ping. Ping.* It was very still. I tried to look her in the face. There was no panic. She wasn't crying, she wasn't shouting, she wasn't moving.

I saw how the piece of ice that up to now had borne her weight slowly gave way to the water.

PING.

And she was gone.

SIXTEEN

WHEN A LIFE is reduced to figures, the rest of the world ceases to exist.

Duration of hypothermia:	7 minutes
Body temperature:	83.6°
Pulse/heart rate:	28/min
Blood pressure:	67/34
Saturation	76%
Duration of unconsciousness:	10 hours
Chance of recovery:	<40%

"What does that mean, Brech, chance of recovery less than forty percent?"

"Don't ask, Gideon."

"What does it mean, Brech—talk to me."

"A chance of four out of ten. That's what it means. Don't ask, Gideon."

"*Talk* to me, Brechje: what is four out of ten? Four what? Out of ten what?"

"What do you want to hear?"

"Talk to me, Brechje, talk to me."

I'd put my head across her thighs. We were sitting on uncomfortable wooden chairs at the foot of Lizzy's bed. Whenever I became restless, she took my head in her hands and guided it back onto her lap. I closed my eyes. Like a gong in the cathedral of Arles, it reverberated in my head: *Ping. Ping.*

I opened my eyes. The thin green line of Lizzy's heartbeat displayed a regular peak in between interminably long intervals.

Bleep. Line. *Bleep.*

What does it mean when the heartbeat is regular—even when it's so slow? Does that have any influence on the four out of ten? Is she closer to the four than the ten?

"Talk to me."

I shifted my position so that I could see all the apparatus at once: the respirator, the drip, the monitor that recorded pulse and temperature.

"If you knew everything that you could possibly know at this moment," Brechje spoke softly, "and if all your questions were answered; if you could determine all the data and make all the numbers concrete; if you understood all the figures and the relationship of each figure to every other figure, and could interpret each percentage in relation to zero or a hundred—what certainty would that give you, Gideon? Would you have more hope or less? Would it give you something to hold on to? Would it give you peace of mind?"

Lizzy lay in the oversize hospital bed, enveloped in foil like a baked potato ready for the barbecue, the tubes and electrodes connecting her to a system that temporarily postponed her death—or her life. All the blood had drained from her face, and her eyes were dark circles; her lips were cold and blue.

"Why isn't Raya here?"

"Jelle's on the phone."

"Is there any news?"

"I'll ask him." Brechje started to get up, but I pulled her back.

"No, let me lie here a little longer."

I put my head back on her lap. She stroked my hair with one hand; with the other she held on to Lizzy's foot.

"Is she cold?"

"No, she's warm. Lukewarm. She's lukewarm."

"Talk to me."

"I am talking to you, Gideon. I'll go on talking to you. My father used to talk to me when I couldn't sleep. He talked to me the way I'm talking to you. I often had trouble sleeping when I was little; I couldn't understand why the world was so different from the way it looked to me. At night, lying in bed, I thought about the things I hadn't understood during the day. Then he came in and sat next to my bed and talked to me.

(PROFESSOR KALMA was a great physicist. So great that for twenty years he had narrowly missed getting the Nobel Prize. Failure takes many forms. I read somewhere that the daughters of successful fathers are more likely to succeed than the daughters of ordinary fathers. Brechje worked in her father's lab, but she would never achieve the same heights as her father. Her work involved processing the data on other people's research. Not that you don't have to have brains to do that kind of work, determining the significance of all the incoming pluses and minuses. Brechje was good at her job.)

"MY FATHER told me about the fourteen angels around my bed. Do you know that song: 'When at night I go to sleep, fourteen angels watch do keep...'? He told me that angels really do exist; we can't see them with our eyes, but we can feel them. I believed him. There were so many things in my life that I could feel, even though I couldn't see them. The existence of fourteen angels around my bed seemed just as logical to me as the existence of the stars in the sky—which I'd never seen either."

(BRECHJE'S MOM had died very young, after a freak accident: the front wheel of her bike had caught in a hole in the road. Is that something else that might affect your chances of being successful, whether your mother lived or died? I'm sure it would affect your sense of well-being, or rather the lack of it. Success is something outside yourself. Well-being comes from inside. It's as close to you as a clubfoot.)

"GO ON TALKING."

"Not so long ago some results came in from the Christina Hospital. They'd been studying electromagnetic fields in the Children's ICU, because the equipment seemed to be more prone to failure than was normal on the basis of the statistics. What they discovered was that some of the children were surrounded by a magnetic field at seven places around their bed, and that this was what was causing the disturbances. When they went to process the data, they discovered a connection: these children were more likely to recover. What's more, in each case the inexplicable hitch in the electrical equipment was just enough to tip the scales in the right direction."

My head was getting heavier and heavier, I kept my eyes tightly shut and waded through a landscape filled with white angels' wings.

"Is that really true?"

"What difference does it make, Gideon? Just try to sleep."

She stood up and slid a pillow under my head. Then she disappeared behind the curtain and I descended into a restless sleep.

(I HAD LEARNED from my father that we are allowed to blame life for the fact that we are alive. No doubt he had his reasons. When he and his mother came back to Holland he was eight years old, just under fifty pounds, and couldn't read or write. That's all he ever told me, but he told me that a thousand times. Eight years old. Just under fifty pounds. Illiterate.

He was put in the first grade and was cold-shouldered for seven years. He certainly must be a very stupid boy, the teacher said, and gave him another rap across the knuckles with the ruler. I heard that a thousand times, too.

My father wanted to be an architect: he drew well and liked math. And he was good with his hands. When he left grade school he was fifteen and no longer had to attend school. His mother apprenticed him to a carpenter: the money came in handy. He worked himself up to foreman, developed back problems, and ended up managing the local branch of a do-it-yourself chain.

Failure takes many forms.)

"They just picked Raya up from the boat."
Brechje squatted down next to me and whispered in my ear.
"How?"
"By helicopter. She's on her way to Porto."
"Is it true, what you just said?"
"Yes, it's true."
"Thank God."
After that I fell into unfathomable depths.

(They say that everything is white underneath the ice. They say that the black water appears white, that the roof of the ice is white, that everything you see is shrouded in a white mist. They say that the hole is a black spot, which is strange: danger is white, rescue is black.

They say that when you're drowning you see a thousand different colors. A blue sky full of fluttering apple blossom petals. They say that it's a gentle death, that you hear music, that you think you're back in paradise. They say that it's the most beautiful death.

By the time the firemen arrived, she'd been under the ice for half a lifetime. The divers were in the water in no time. And then it took another half a lifetime. Nurses were waiting with a stretcher and a thermal blanket. Then the diver surfaced and waded through the frozen pond to the shore like an icebreaker. He was carrying Lizzy in his arms, the plastic bag with bread crusts still clutched in her hand. White coats bent over her, wrapped her in foil, connected her to machines.

I looked into my daughter's face, from which all life had disappeared. There was no strain. There was no fear. She wasn't dead. She had entered a white world.)

ON THE DIVIDING LINE between two worlds, I heard footsteps approaching. The rustle of wings. Light fell on my closed eyelids: the curtain was pulled aside.

"Extreme bradycardia," someone mumbled.

"Eighty-six-point-one. Not bad," said a tall angel.

"Support the vital functions until she's warmed up," said another angel.

"We can discontinue the sedative," the tall angel spoke again.

"Pulse is thirty-six, but stable."

"Then keep the sedative going. Until the transfer."

The angels disappeared behind the curtain through which they had come.

"WAKE UP, GIDEON. Coffee."

Jelle had stayed behind after the doctors left and now he was shaking my shoulder gently. I had a terrible pain in my neck. The pillow Brechje had left for me had fallen to the floor. It must have been the middle of the night: the light in the hallway was faint, and in the nurses' cubicle I saw flickering images on a television screen.

"Is Raya here?"

"She's on her way."

"Where's Brech?"

"She went home to shower."

"What time is it?"

"Six o'clock. In the morning."

A wet washcloth was shoved into my face and I was handed a clean shirt. Jelle led the way out of the ICU, past the swinging doors where we left our white coats, down a long corridor with doors on either side, which I assumed concealed moribund patients, and then to the elevator which took us downstairs to the central reception hall of the hospital and the coffee shop.

The smell of cigarettes and fresh croissants made my stomach churn.

I was unable to swallow the breakfast that Jelle brought me from the cafeteria. I took a sip of coffee from the cardboard cup and ran to the rest room to spew the gall that my body had produced in the last twenty-four hours. When I got back to our table, I saw that Jelle had obtained a sugar solution from the nurses' station, which he made me drink.

"If you go on like this, you'll fall flat on your face. Get a grip on yourself, Gideon. Your daughter needs you."

"Where are we now?" I asked shakily. I fought against the fear and desperation that seemed to be forcing the gall back up into my throat.

"Sometime during the morning Lizzy will be warmed up. She's up to almost eighty-eight degrees now. When she's reached her normal body temperature, they'll take her off the sedative, so we can see how she's come through."

"What do we know right now?"

"Right now we don't know anything. She's totally dependent on the machines. There's no telling which bodily functions will be able to carry on their own. We'll have to wait and see."

"Wait and see? Christ, Jelle, I'm so tired."

"The transfer is at eight o'clock. They're going to keep her asleep at least until then. And now no more crap, Gideon. Come on, we're going outside."

W E   D R O V E   through the darkness in the direction of the beach. In the beam of our headlights a rabbit scuttled off into the dunes. I followed the animal with my gaze (I thought that rabbits hibernated) and saw a light over the top of the dunes. The neon letters on the roof read: *Duinzicht Guesthouse*. I told Jelle that was where we were headed.

It was going to be a freezing-cold day. A day for skating. A day for hot chocolate.

We ordered two Beerenburgs from the waiter, who was busy with the breakfast tables. Jelle was a northerner, too.

"What did your dad die of?" I asked, as we leaned against the bar of the deserted hotel. Behind us, the waiter was taking his time setting a table for four. The sleepy face of a woman appeared at the door of the kitchen. They didn't like the look of us; that much was clear.

The Beerenburg went down the hatch, and we ordered another one.

"Cardiac arrest," Jelle answered with a grin, "not very original. During a congress in Ghent."

"At least it wasn't that far away," I said vaguely.

"Jesus, Gideon! Don't you have anything better to talk about than my father?" There was the same old annoyance in his voice.

"Talk to me, Jelle."

"About my father?"

"I have a father, too," was all I could think of, "and I'm a father, too."

"I   W A S   T H E   O N E   who answered the phone," he began, after we'd been walking along the beach for a while. "Mom was sitting on the couch reading a magazine. It was early in the evening. The telephone rang, I picked up the receiver, and a woman with a Flemish accent asked me if I was Jelle Ripperda, the son of Djoeke Ripperda, etc., etc. Then you know what's coming. I don't remember exactly what else the Flemish lady said, only that he was dead, and that there was no need to rush. I remember thinking that was a rather morbid kind of reassurance.

After I put the phone down, I turned around to look at my mother and—damn it all—I had a grin on my face that I couldn't for the life of me get rid of. "Mother," I said, "Dad is dead.'"

(AS A LITTLE GIRL, Raya had developed a tendency to lose a few drops just before going to the toilet. It wasn't deliberate; one day it just happened, and after that it never went away. That premature pee sent her into fits of laughter because it was so asinine, and sometimes that made her wet her pants. Even now she often giggled when she had to go. Usually at parties or the movies.)

"THERE'S A PHOTOGRAPH," Jelle went on, "taken on the gangplank of a Speedo boat. One of those touristy photos. There was my father, young, smartly dressed, self-confident. And there I was next to him and a step or two behind, in new clothes we'd bought that morning at Peek and Cloppenburg: a ludicrous grown-up suit for little boys, with a tie and black patent leather shoes. I must have been about five or six, at the most. It was our first 'Father's Day'—that's what he called it. He'd dreamed it up to show everyone what a good father he was. Once a year we went off together, just the two of us: first the zoo and then a boat trip through the canals, or else we spent the day at an amusement park and had French fries at Van der Valk's. Apparently lots of his colleagues did the same thing with their sons, so it probably wasn't even his idea.

"Mother and I were looking for a photograph to put on the obituary card to hand out at the cremation ceremony; she already had a poem for the back, by one of her interesting friends. That's when I came across that picture. And suddenly it hit me: what was it you were trying to tell me? My father's hand isn't resting on my shoulder. His gaze, his whole body is directed toward the camera. 'Look!' the photo is saying, 'when you grow up you can become as successful as I am, and earn so much money that one afternoon you can go out and buy a whole new outfit for your son. Look! I may be your father, but I'm not holding on to you, I'm not taking your hand, not even on this wobbly gangplank. You're perfectly capable of walking alone.' That's what he's saying: 'You're perfectly capable of walking alone. And I enjoy being with you, in your monkey suit, that one day a year.'"

THERE WAS A STUBBLY BEARD on my friend's face from the past twenty-four hours, his sandy hair was graying, there were crow's-feet in the corners of his eyes. His skin was ashen from the past night, but I guessed from the past few years as well. At thirty-five the outside world sees you as an adult, even though you feel as if only yesterday you were still wet behind the ears. Barely equipped to cope with life in earnest.

(I AM THE SAME AGE as my father was in my earliest memories. We're sitting under the slanting window of the attic in the duplex on Anemoonstraat. My father's oily hair is combed straight back; he smells of cigarettes and cooking oil and strong soap. For the first time he's taken me up to the attic, where he spends his time when he's not working. We leaf through colorful magazines with illustrations of castles and country homes along the Vecht. He explains how they were built and tells me all about dovetail joints and wind stops and stretchers and headers. I listen to the words as if they're some kind of incantation, and I admire him because he knows about such things. He uses tracing paper to make scale drawings of all those magnificent houses he's cut out. Then he starts building: using cigar boxes, matchboxes, wire, papier-mâché. I get to watch but I'm not allowed to touch anything. He says I still don't know how to stay inside the lines.)

I GUESS that's the way nature intended it to be: we have to kill our parents before we can become parents ourselves. You have to get rid of that first version of yourself—the version to whom your mother says "Ah, my boy," and your father shows his unfulfilled dreams—in order to make room for that other version of yourself: the one someone will one day call Daddy. If you don't, then you'll spend the rest of your life juggling those three variants of yourself: the child, the parent, and another being that you hope is your autonomous "self." They're bound to start jostling one another, until one of them slips from your grasp and goes crashing to the ground.

IN THE MILKY WHITE morning light we returned in silence to what I had tried to banish from my head during the past few hours. It was not only my daughter who was poised at the edge of the abyss; it was also the third variant of myself. You become attached to a child, but also to fatherhood. Her life-and-death struggle had to do with part of my life—or death. It was very much in my interest that she should live.

AT 10:48 A.M. MY DAUGHTER, Lizzy Mira Salomon, thawed. She awoke from her artificial sleep, opened her eyes, said weakly, "Hi, Daddy," and after this exertion closed her eyes again for another twenty-four hours.

"It's quite astounding how resilient children are," said the young doctor on duty as she studied Lizzy's chart. "I wouldn't have bet a bottle of wine that this little gal would make it."

And I'd have broken that bottle of wine over your head if you'd said that before, I thought, but then I was reminded of Djoeke Ripperda: the knowledge that I could relinquish my vengeance made me feel more charitable.

And besides: Lizzy was alive. And I was recovering.

SEVENTEEN

RAYA MIRA WAS BACK, but she wasn't talking to me.

She seated herself on a high stool next to Lizzy's bed and told her stories: about seas that were first blue and then green, foreshadowing a storm, and about clouds as fluffy as cotton candy that turn bright pink when the sun goes down. She told her about flying fish in the night that skim the surface of the water like so many lamps, and about dolphins that swim alongside the boat. She told her about a rainbow that during a lull had fallen over backward into the water, and about the geese that flew north while she was sailing south.

When Lizzy's bed went from the hospital to our living room, Raya brought her stool home with her and went on telling stories. There were mermaids who followed their beloved across the seven seas, and a pirate ship that pursued them at night but was invisible during the day. She told her how every night a white dove returned to the mast, even when they were several days away from land. She told her that a large bird had come to get her and bring her home. She told her how she traveled back in time, from the hot summer in the south to the winter in the north, where her daughter was waiting for her.

She wasn't writing either.

She bought a blue spruce and decorated it for Christmas. She baked wreaths of pink and white meringue and hung them in the tree on ribbons. She made mulled wine and hot lemonade, lit candles in the living room, and sang "Silent Night" for Lizzy. She never left her daughter's side.

Raya Mira was silent—but it was a different kind of silence than before she left. I was used to her silences; it wasn't always clear to me what was going on inside her, but I knew that one day she would share with me the fruits of that silence. This time I didn't have that same confidence: Raya Mira was silent, but she was not writing. She was brooding.

I turned to my daughter.

"Lizzy, what do you miss the most?" I asked her.

She had been confined to bed for over a month: the small body had been totally exhausted, which had led to complications and, in turn, to medication that had made her sick. Now the year was coming to a close and she was slowly regaining her strength. She still wasn't allowed outside.

"Trees," came the prompt answer.

I threw my photocase over my shoulder and plunged into the winter landscape, in search of the most beautiful tree in the woods for my daughter. I found it in Appelscha. There, among the sickly conifers, a young copper beech had taken root on the dead trunk of a predecessor. I hung the photo over her bed.

"The clouds" was my next assignment, then "the birds" and "the moon and the stars."

With my Mamiya I recaptured for Lizzy the ground she had lost because of me. It was a race against time, an attempt not only to recover all the pieces of her life, but also to recover her, as she had been.

As we had been together, I would say now.

"THAT WON'T HAPPEN," I was told by the doctor, whom I had asked to see. It was the young woman who wouldn't have bet a bottle of wine on Lizzy's recovery. She wasn't as bad as I initially thought.

"The fact is, Lizzy's lost part of her memory," she said with certainty, "and in this case it's not going to come back. Because she was in shock for a time, she probably can't even remember those minutes on the ice, let alone the time under the ice. In fact, due to the sedative we administered, the entire recovery period is probably a blank page in her memory. Call it a coma, if you like: no stimulus of any kind reached her consciousness during that twenty-four-hour period."

"What does that do to a child?" I asked her. I couldn't accept that a "blank page" is really blank: you can't cut a piece out of someone's life, just because her brain didn't record it. "Her frontal lobe, her cerebral cortex, her DNA, for Christ's sake! *Some* part of her must have registered something during the twenty-four hours that she was unconscious?"

I told her about my father's lost memories, which had marked him for life. You could call that a blank page, too: the events have been erased from the blackboard. But that doesn't mean that the effect of those events has been erased: it continues to nag, on a different level maybe, but it's always there in the back of your mind.

"Falling through the ice is probably quite different from what your father went through," the doctor said curtly. "And besides, he did consciously experience the events themselves; it's the memories that he's buried. That's an entirely different story. Lizzy will come through this just fine, and what she doesn't remember...well, it doesn't make for very pleasant memories. I'm tempted to say, Just be happy that she didn't consciously experience it."

I gave it another try. "But what does it *do* to a child?"

"It doesn't do anything," she said, as she shoved her chair back from the desk. "Children are made of rubber. Their resilience—especially their mental resilience—is far greater than we can even imagine. I think I already told you that."

This time I would cheerfully have hit her over the head with that bottle of wine. She was even worse than I thought.

In film terminology, there is something called "zero time." This is the time between the end of one scene and the beginning of the next: in a film story it might be a minute or a day or a whole lifetime. From one minute to the next we leap forward in time: at the splice a young man becomes a graybeard, or a little girl a young lady. That leap is believable because we have learned to fill in the zero time. In a fraction of a second—the time it takes to tape one filmed image to another—we can visualize the period in between.

It's not about reality, and it doesn't even matter what that period looked like. We know that it's there and we fill it in for ourselves.

According to the doctor, the zero time that Lizzy raced through was no more than ordinary Scotch tape: a transparent scrap of celluloid joining before and after. I was convinced that the time in between really did exist, and that we could find a way to fill it in. I wanted to give her back the memory that had been lost.

February came and the thaw set in. I rented a small wheelchair from the medical center: it had a red, yellow, and blue metal frame and Miffy rabbits on the seat. Lizzy was wrapped in a blanket and wheeled outdoors. She was as weak as a kitten, but had regained enough strength to be able to face the waning winter cold.

I put a bag of old bread crusts in her lap.

"Where are we going?" she asked bravely—I could see the fear in her eyes.

"We're going for a walk," I said, and I started walking. To my relief, she asked no more questions. But when we turned the corner of the Wenckebachlaan and the pond behind Little Heaven came into sight, the blood drained from her face.

"Do you recognize it?" I asked.

Lizzy nodded, but said nothing.

"How much do you remember?"

She looked straight ahead, across the pond that had almost taken her life. There was still some ice on the surface; it was full of leaves and branches, and the scrawny ducks paddled around jauntily in large black holes.

"Nothing," she said, and pushed the bag of bread resolutely aside.

"Then we're going to make a memory for you," I said, and I placed a small, brand-new camera in her lap. She looked up at me inquiringly.

"If you can't remember anything, sweetie, then you'll never be able to accept what happened. You'll always be afraid of water, of ice, of ducks, of winter. Of life."

"What's mem-o-ry, Daddy?"

"Memory is imagination."

"What's imag-i-nation, Daddy?"

"Pictures in your head, Lizzy. Pictures of what happened when you fell through the ice, all the things you don't remember exactly."

"I don't want pictures in my head!" She put her hands over her eyes.

"Do you want to make up stories," I tried, "stories for in your head? Pictures to go with the stories you make up yourself?"

"Mermaids," she asked from behind her hands, "do they fit in your head, too?"

"No problem," I said brightly. I felt she was beginning to get my drift. "Were there mermaids in your head when you went through the ice?"

Then the door banged shut again. The expensive, brand-new little camera was shoved crossly behind the bag of bread.

Bite your tongue, I told myself; this is a one-off.

I helped her out of the wheelchair. We left the bag of bread behind on the Miffy cushion, but I dropped the camera into my pocket. I picked her up and walked over to the weeping willow where she'd seen the ducks. There weren't any ducks there now; they were all swimming around in the black opening in the ice.

"Looks like there's enough to eat again," I said cheerily. Lizzy didn't answer; the ducks no longer seemed to interest her. We walked on to the remains of the wooden bridge. That's where I had seen her for the last time, poking at the ice with her spade. Then she suddenly jumped down, and pointed out a hole in the rotten foundations.

"Look, Daddy"—she pointed—"isn't it pretty!"

Deep inside the black wood a small puddle had formed, no larger than a fist, and now it was teeming with tiny creatures. Larvae, frogs' eggs—I was never any good at biology—I guess they're called *organisms*. In the sunlight that slanted through the bare trees, they were illuminated like fireflies at dusk. I handed her the camera. She looked up at me with a question in her eyes.

"Go on"—I nodded encouragingly—"go on, if you think it's pretty."

She took a photo and she was beaming when she handed back the camera.

"I saw them then, too," she murmured, "all kinds of little animals. Just like little lamps."

We circled the water until we got to a landing stage that must have been used to moor rowboats. Lizzy lay down on her tummy and took photos through the wide gaps between the planks. The ice underneath was white as snow, with thin black lines where dirt and dust had settled. For a long time she watched the ducks swimming around in the hole in the ice, until one of them dived under the surface of the water, leaving behind a widening series of circles. Then she clicked. That night, in the darkroom, the first images took shape, images of the world in which she had found herself, a world of light and dark, tiny lights in a vacuum, circles in an ice hole, black water.

"Is this what you saw," I asked the next morning as she bent over the prints, "or is there something missing?"

"That's it," she said thoughtfully. "That's what I saw. There was lots of black and white. But lots of colors, too."

She didn't know exactly which colors, and she couldn't describe what it looked like. Just colors—that's what we had to find.

It's usually in the cutting room that a filmmaker discovers what kind of a job he did on the set. That's when the real work begins. No matter how clear he was in his mind about the development of the story line and the weight each scene ought to have, the images do not reveal their significance until they're in the right sequence, the right context. Until they're fixed in time, in the story, in the course of events.

It's the same thing with memory. Creating a memory is kindergarten work: you cut and paste and color until you get it right. The repository of our memory has no more significance than all those unmounted feet of celluloid, an accumulation of impressions that you can dip into at will. It's only afterward, when the paste has dried, that you can say, That's the way it was. Or should have been.

This is what I remember. The first time, I took Lizzy to the beach to see the setting sun. I asked her whether those were the colors: the red of the clouds, the gray of the sea. But they weren't. Then we went to the park, where the early spring flowers were in bloom, and to a tulip nursery; it was all lovely, but it wasn't what she meant. I took her to the opera, to the deep-sea aquarium, and we took a couple of turns in the illuminated Ferris wheel. Lizzy shook her head apologetically. Thanks, Daddy, I had a really good time, but that wasn't it.

"What on earth are you looking for?" Raya asked when we got back from a visit to the old restored planetarium. I had high hopes—the vault of the sky cobalt blue, with gold stars and the moon—but that wasn't it either.

Raya looked at me. I said nothing.

Spring finally arrived and the garden was a cloud of lilac and blue. Over the years Raya had planted so many cuttings of the rhododendron that everything was covered in a blaze of deep violet flowers set against dark green foliage. The other plants had either not survived or had ended up on the compost heap. Neither one of us had a green thumb. I brought down the boxes of rosé from the attic and put the white wine in the shed to cool. Raya put on a heavy sweater and settled herself on the deck, where the wooden beams now reminded me of the rotting foundations of the bridge near Little Heaven. We'd never be real do-it-yourselfers either.

We drank to that and were silent. There was a strong hint of spring in the air.

OUR LIFE RETURNED TO NORMAL. Raya had gone back to scribbling in her notebooks. Lizzy was growing up. In my free time I'd take her to see an exhibition of Jackson Pollock's paintings, or sculptures by Appel. It was an offshoot of our quest for colors, and now part of responsible child rearing. It was like feeding the ducks, only now with a big girl.

We had stopped talking about it.

And yet there were nights full of unrest when I'd wake with a jolt and end up in the darkroom, bent over my contact prints with the smell of chemicals in my nose, picking up first this paper, then the other. The darkroom has a soothing effect on me; I can retreat to my own territory, with only my thoughts for company. The ritual of the various procedures—paper, trays of liquid, the manipulation of light and shadow, the soft ticking of the clock— makes me briefly a magician in my own universe. It had a calming effect.

But I was still plagued by the same question, the question that made me wake up with a start: what was it that she'd seen, what was that image she could not recall? I picked up the nine negatives she'd shot that afternoon in the park, and tried one variation after the other: more contrast, other freezes, other filters, a different mask. I had stopped asking whether I'd gotten it right this time: the color wasn't there.

It was on one of those nights that Raya appeared. The umpteenth series of Lizzy's photos was hanging on the line to dry, and although it wasn't necessary, I'd kept the light dim. I was peering at nine blurred prints in the red half-light. Then I caught sight of Raya's face: she never entered the darkroom without a reason, and she must have come in quietly while I was absorbed in some procedure. She was sitting on the high stool near the door, and she too was looking at the dripping line.

She handed me a glass of whisky. "Nice framing," she said.

"You've seen them all before," I answered offhandedly. Her presence infringed on my territory, but a sense of relief predominated. That she had wanted to come. She was at last looking at them with me.

"But it's still your framing," she continued. I resolved to be on my guard. "It's your hands, Gideon, your hands that are manipulating her images. It's your evaluation that determines the gray tones. The fact that you're doing the printing is her limitation, the falsification of her memory. What you've taken on here is a never-ending task: every single time, the rock of

her memory will fall back onto your own head. You're project-
ing onto her an image that's complete, filled out from edge
to edge. The image she saw wasn't filled in. It had no bounda-
ries. It had no frame. It coincided with what she saw. She *was*
that submerged life hanging here on your wash line in nine
parts."

"So what is the meaning of this image-in-nine-parts that Lizzy
gave me? The water, the circles, the ice, the spots on her retina—
is none of that of any importance? Does it mean that her whole
story about blacks and whites and colors is empty? All just theoretical conjecturing?"

"That's exactly what it is. In every print we see your hand, your
limitations, your choice. Your style, if you like. That young doctor, the one who nearly drove you crazy, wasn't far off the mark.
You can aestheticize Lizzy's experience until you're blue in the
face—in black and white and all the colors of the rainbow—you'll
still be none the wiser. It'll still be your interpretation of ' er
emptiness."

I went over to the filing cabinet and opened the drawer
where I'd put her photos. I spread out the various prints of that
one photo in which Lizzy had recorded the circles in the water.
On reflection, I was moved more than anything else by the in-
nocence with which she had set about the task, the almost total
absence of contrast, resulting in only the vaguest suspicion of
circles. And yet it was my favorite, and I explained this to Raya:
as you bend over the countless variations on that image of
vague circles against a black field, it's as if you're being sucked
into the vortex. As if you're staring into a kaleidoscope that
keeps producing the same image, but with minute variations.
But what made it so intriguing was the fact that I never tired
of it. Every time I looked at it, it evoked a new thought, a new
association.

"Don't you see? That's it," said Raya.

With a sigh, I poured us both another whisky. And I was reminded of why I cherished the solitude of the darkroom. Words,
words, words.

"Gideon, use your head and stop listening to that bleeding
heart of yours! Can't you see that for Lizzy there's never going
to be anything except what you yourself describe? The memory
or the experience or the images—whatever word you use for her
blank page—will reveal itself to her again and again. It can't
be fixed. She'll grow up with it. It will become part of her. It's
like the butterfly that won't be pinned down without giving up
its life."

"Am I trying to pin her down?" I asked, startled.

"More likely yourself." She gave me a kiss and ran out of the
darkroom.

WHEN I WOKE UP THE NEXT MORNING, I felt
that the bed next to me was cold and hadn't been slept in. The
hall light was on, Lizzy appeared to be fast asleep, and in the
kitchen the coffee was already in the thermos. I went back to
the bedroom, pulled on a sweater under my bathrobe, and went
outside. Raya was sitting on the deck. She had on the same clothes
she'd been wearing the day before. The hands around the coffee
mug were covered in soil, and her short nails were black. She
smiled a tired smile when she saw me standing in the door of the
kitchen.

My God, I thought.

The backyard was a barren expanse of mud. With manic
precision, every single rhododendron had been dug up and
thrown onto a huge pile. The soil had been turned over and
then raked, until there wasn't a single blade of grass still standing, not a single root left in the ground. Bags of fresh potting
soil had been strewn over the surface; the hose she had used to
water the garden was still dripping. The blossoms of the felled

rhododendrons lay piled up against the fence like a stranded cloud.

Next to her on the deck was a small pile of cuttings.

"I was sick of the sight of flower blossoms," she said apologetically.

"My God," I said, "are you out of your mind?"

"No, my darling"—she looked up in surprise—"of course not. I'm just starting all over again."

EIGHTEEN

IN THE MONTHS THAT FOLLOWED, Raya retreated
to the attic to unpack the boxes that had remained untouched
since the move. It was a cold, bleak summer. As the stove hummed
in the background, I taught Lizzy the fundamentals of chess, we
ate baked apples with vanilla custard, and we turned the heat up
high. After that first exuberant overture of spring, it was as if time
had stood still: as if nature had squandered all its energy before
summer had even arrived. The leaves shriveled on their branches,
the roots rotted in the ground, the birds were still. That year summer was not a season in its own right, but only a lull in time, somewhere between spring and fall.

*Summer makes no promises, at best it has to keep them. After nine
sluggish months, a cloudless sky is not a favor, but an acquired right. Of
all the seasons, summer is the least enviable.*

Raya had started leaving me notes again. I'd missed them. There
was something reassuring about her scraps of paper, like this one,
pinned to the tea cozy. The familiarity of her thoughts had gradually exceeded the intimacies we shared. We had been together almost six years.

ONE OF THE BIGGEST MISTAKES of my life was not
saving her notes. I know now that they were the most important

thing she ever gave me: footnotes to our life, the topography of her brain. But it all began in such an offhand, almost trivial way, that I didn't realize how important they were until it was too late, until the first chapters of her biography were already at the bottom of the wastebasket.

"The notes you leave for me—do you write them down in your notebook?" I asked cautiously, after I had realized my thoughtlessness. She was discreet enough not to ask what I did with her notes. As a rule I took them to the darkroom, reread them and then, after a while, put them into a drawer until spring-cleaning time came around and they ended up in the wastepaper basket. No, she said, she didn't copy them into her notebook: the notes were for me, the notebooks for herself or for Lizzy. She preferred to keep them separate. And besides, she liked the idea that they were part of a loose-leaf system: "I'm always a little wary of my own words. When I say them out loud or work them out on paper, they seem so irrefutable that it's absurd."

"Irrefutable doesn't necessarily mean absurd, Raya," I held forth. "Shouldn't you have the courage to stand up for what you think, or feel, or do?"

She gave me a teasing look and then said maliciously, "I know you throw them away, and that's a great comfort to me."

IN THE SUNROOM there was a tattered cardboard moving box filled to the brim with negatives and stray photographs of our life: the house, barbecues with friends, trips to the beach. It annoyed me that the box just sat there, that it hadn't been sorted out, that the photos hadn't been pasted in. Every single envelope that came back from Hema or the lab disappeared into that box. Undated. Unsorted. Sometimes even unseen.

"Life isn't a loose-leaf system," I said.

"This doesn't represent our life," she said.

It's trivialities like this that tell you the foundations are shifting.

But there's no way of seeing it when you're smack in the middle of it. The way she tossed pictures into a box hit me hard. I was the one who took those photos: images were my language, my life. And that wasn't all: those snapshots—no matter how unattractive, out of focus, or meaningless—represented the life that we shared. Her lack of consideration wasn't only irritating; it went deeper than that.

"There's a flaw in your reasoning, Gideon." And off we went again: I'd brought up the subject of the photos and wham! the fat was in the fire. "Where you go wrong is that you think that order and structure automatically provide stability, give you a grip on life. But look what happens when you turn that around: why does the water in that vase putrefy? And why do the flowers putrefy along with the water? Stability, Gideon, is stagnation. And stagnation leads to disintegration."

"You refuse to commit yourself to anything, Raya. Okay, except for your daughter—that's the only area where you're unconditional. The rest of your life is surrounded by ifs and ands and clever asides. You're absolutely certain about everything—except yourself."

(THE IDEA *that there is such a thing as stability or certainty is life's greatest pitfall. Even searching for it is asking for trouble, because either you'll be deprived of any grip on life or you'll deprive yourself of it. You said that dedication—committing yourself—is different. Dedication is letting go. Dedication demands pruning and growth, or maybe that should be the other way around. I found this one in the shed, on my mother's Miele, next to the colored laundry.*)

"COME UPSTAIRS WITH ME," Raya said. Brechje had been by that morning to pick Lizzy up. They were going to the circus and afterward they'd have French fries and cotton candy, and Lizzy would stay overnight. The house was empty and quiet; we were seldom home alone, just the two of us. So seldom that I found it hard to get used to. I felt as lost as a balloon without a string.

Carrying a tray with tea glasses in one hand and a bottle of brandy in the other, I mounted the pull-down ladder to the attic. I seldom went up there; I didn't like the place. The smell of roll-your-own tobacco and cooking oil and unfulfilled longing hung between the beams. I stuck my head above the ladder and saw my Raya sitting in the middle of piles of paper: letters, postcards held together by a worn-out rubber band, old report cards. A photograph album.

I handed her the tea, with a splash of brandy. In her lap lay Annetje Slik's album: the name was written across the front in an endearing scrawl: *Annetje Slik 1960–1970*. It looked like an epitaph.

She slid closer to me and opened the album: gray cardboard and drab snapshots from another world, another life. Each photo was accompanied by the particulars, in her mother's best school handwriting: *Street party on the queen's birthday* (Raya, at six or so, looking bewildered with a silly crown on her head); *Mother's birthday: 55!* (old faces above a cake with whipped-cream frosting, Raya in an impossible dress on someone's lap); *Summer 1965* (posing in the sandbox next to an array of much too perfect mud pies). Silently she leafed through the album, which had apparently been compiled with great care by Gonnie Slik. The effect on Raya seemed to be mainly one of sadness.

"This, my darling, is the reason why I have such an aversion to pasting in photos."

I went on leafing through the album of her childhood, the only period in her life that was well documented, and I had to acknowledge the cheerlessness of it all. The faces. The captions. The festive moments.

"Hey, our life isn't that pathetic, is it?"

"As long as the past is lying carelessly in a shoe box, you can at least pretend that there's some room to maneuver," Raya said, ignoring my irony. "Once you select the snapshots, paste them in, and write the captions, the book of your past is closed. And as soon as you do that, a part of yourself is irrevocably lost. You've pasted your own past into a book—outside yourself, beyond yourself."

I pointed to the scrawl on the cover of the album: "It really does look like an epitaph," I remarked.

"Once you pin down intentions, even good intentions, Gideon, everything's up in the air again."

"But you can turn that around, Raya. A lot of intentions—good intentions included—don't become visible until you put them in context. Life never gets past the noncommittal, no-obligation stage if you're afraid to make choices: to select, discard, cut, and paste. Not until then do you get a story; not until then does the meaning come floating to the surface."

"You're right," she said, "but the dangerous part of any story is the conclusion. That's what appeals to me in the thousand-and-one-nights stories: Scheherazade told her stories shamelessly, without head or tail, her sole aim was to exorcise death. The danger in our stories is that we try to name things, in order to control them. We use words to exorcise life. We're afraid of it. We hate open endings."

In a corner of the attic a small petroleum stove was humming softly. Under the drafty eaves, it seemed even more like fall than outside. We drank tea and snuggled closer together, browsing through the paper remains of her past. A pile of postcards went flying into the trash bag. "Amazing how much junk gets caught in the dragnet." She smiled. Fascinated, I went on leafing through the photo album. Something fell out: a photo of two little girls. One of them was clearly Raya; the other face was unusually large and uneven.

I showed her the picture. "Your mother must have forgotten this one."

She looked up and shook her head thoughtfully. "No, she didn't forget. She refused to paste it in."

"Who's the other girl?"

"This is exactly what I meant."

"So who's the other girl?"

Raya took the photograph from my hand and stared at it intently. "Edda," I heard her say. "Edda. Aka. Aka."

Mumbling to herself, she looked for the road leading back into her memories, as if she were sitting there with the map in her hand and repeating *Oldorp* and *Holwinde*. I followed her with my eyes. She had come to virgin territory, unknown to me, perhaps land that she herself had not yet explored.

"Where are you, my girl?" I asked after a while.

Then she was back in the drafty attic, smiling at me. She stood up, went down the ladder, and came back with an ashtray and cigarettes.

"In need of moral support?"

"In need of moral support." She nodded and lit a cigarette.

"Aka came to stay with us when I was four or five. My mother and I were still living with my grandparents. I guess I was bored, or maybe it was something else, something I'm only now beginning to understand. You see, as a child I must have had the feeling that my mother married her Spanish lover because of me, and that it was because of me that she later moved back in with her parents. It wasn't the kind of life that she'd dreamed of, I'm sure of that. Gonnie Slik had other plans for her future. She wanted to become a midwife. My existence kept her from doing what she wanted to do. I turned her into a mother. And I must have sensed that.

"Aka lived in my grandparents' cellar, surrounded by rhubarb compote and sprouting potatoes. That was her punishment. She was a naughty girl. If I spilled milk on the tablecloth, I gave her a smack. If I got my Sunday-best dress dirty, or wet my pants, Aka was the one who paid the price. I used to spend all afternoon down in the cellar, having a serious word with Aka, and explaining to her just how she was expected to behave. But I also stayed with her because she was afraid of the dark, afraid of being alone in that damp cellar, afraid of the spiders and mice that lived there. I took her in my arms and sang songs to comfort her.

"My mother didn't approve. I started spending more and more time on the cellar steps. I ate my sandwiches there; I read my picture books out loud. She heard me talking, heard me berating the imaginary girl who lived in the cellar, heard me crying because I'd been too hard on Aka and was sorry. Something that began as a figment of my imagination, because I needed someone to talk to, became a reality. I couldn't get along without Aka, not even for a day. I became the little girl who lived in the cellar.

"My birthday was coming up and my mother decided to organize a party. She'd made a Hansel-and-Gretel house out of pancakes, and invited a little girl over to eat it with me. Ella was a couple of years older and lived on our street. She was retarded. She couldn't even say her own name. She had a thick, Mongoloid tongue, which is why she called herself Edda. Actually she couldn't talk at all, but she was a marvelous listener. My mother's tactics proved successful: Aka disappeared.

"Edda became my new rag doll. Edda was my Aka, but this one was made of flesh and blood. After a while I couldn't get along without her—and she couldn't get along without me. And that began to annoy me: Edda wanted something from me; Edda wanted to be my friend. Aka had been safe: I could practice life on her. I thought that Edda was safe because she couldn't talk. But it turned out that she had needs. It turned out that she needed me. No matter how retarded, she was indeed made of flesh and blood.

"On a hot summer day we went swimming and I tried to drown her. It was pretty naive of me. Edda may have been dumb and retarded, but she was also much bigger and stronger than I was. We were taking turns ducking each other and I tried to hold her head underwater. She struggled. She took a bite out of my shoulder and the water started to turn red. The lifeguard saw it in time. Not long after that, we moved away."

(IF I'D PRESERVED her words in a glass jar, if I'd kept all her notes and filed them carefully—complete with date, where they were found, and the circumstances under which they were written—could I have seen it coming? Could I have read the signs, the rumbling in the interior of the volcano, the tiny squiggle on the seismograph that predicts a future eruption?

With the benefit of hindsight, it's easy; with the benefit of hindsight just about anything can be interpreted in the direction of the ultimate results. And yet, during that chilly summer Raya began to talk. It was a bad omen, but perhaps you could say that, looking back, every omen is bad—and every sign significant. Like Rorschach's butterflies.)

THAT EVENING we celebrated the fact that it was six years since we first met. We reserved a table for two at El Regalo, and looked forward to the fine vintage wines we were going to order. We giggled as we stood in front of the tall mirror, and decked ourselves out. Raya painted her nails red. I felt slightly embarrassed as I watched her putting on her makeup: it had become something intimate. Dressing up for each other was no longer automatic; it had lost its routine quality; it had ceased to be banal. We sat on the toilet with the door ajar, but seduction was surrounded by diffidence.

Between dessert and coffee, we toasted each other. We gave each other a gift. Raya had a litho made of one of the first drawings I'd done of Lizzy: the body of a child curled up like a larva in a cloud of white sheets, her toes in the folds of linen a litter of sightless baby mice.

"It's your best self-portrait," she said.

I'd bought her a laptop. That afternoon, after her story up in the attic, I'd jumped on my bike, gone to the store, and bought her an expensive lightweight laptop that she could take with her wherever she went.

"It's time you started to write the book that's you," I said, suddenly moved. "I forget too much of what you say, and I've thrown away too much of what you've written. I'm asking you to start all over again."

"It's already begun," she said.

NINETEEN

D E A T H E N T E R E D our house when the doorbell rang and I saw a dark figure standing in the door opening, silhouetted against the sunlight.

It was the family doctor.

I had called him. And then forgotten about it. I had called the same way I would have called him first thing in the morning for a repeat prescription. Brief. Businesslike. And then I forgot about it.

"Henk Siebold," said the man into the receiver.

"Salomon," I answered. "Could you come by to sign the death certificate for our daughter."

There was an icy silence on the other end of the line.

"Lizzy," I jogged his memory, "Lizzy Mira Salomon."

There was another long silence.

"What was the address?" the man asked.

"Oude Houtstraat thirty-three," I answered.

"I'll be right there," he said, and the line went dead.

And still it didn't get through to me. The man was coming over, so I made fresh coffee. Raya was taking a shower. It was still early, I don't remember how early, but outside the birds were chirping. They quiet down as soon as human beings take over, when kitchen doors and windows are thrown open and the silence is drowned out by the sounds of a new day, with motorbikes revving up and radios blaring on construction sites.

Now, they were still singing.

After Raya had finished her shower, I changed the sheets on Lizzy's bed. Raya sat in the chair with the small body on her lap. I had opened the window of her bedroom, and the outside air smelled of dampness and leaves.

"We have to close her eyes," Raya said. "I can't get them to close."

I looked at Lizzy. One eye was closed, the other open. She seemed to be winking at me. We put her back on her bed. She was naked; the early warmth of the new day filled all the rooms of the house. Raya covered her with a sheet. In the kitchen I filled two balloons with warm water and closed them with a knot. I placed the water bags on her eyes—one red and one yellow. Then we closed the door.

With one arm full of bedclothes I went to the shed and programmed my mother's old Miele. Not too hot—biological stains set in cotton—and not too cold, or you won't get the poop out.

Then we had coffee on the deck and listened to the monotonous whir of the washer until the doorbell rang. I opened the door, the doctor and I shook hands uncomfortably, and I led the way to Lizzy's room. He looked surprised when he saw the swags and streamers in the hall and the heart-shaped wreath of balloons on her bedroom door.

"It's her birthday today," I said apologetically. "She's five."

For a moment we stood wordlessly at the foot of her bed in the bluish light of the curtains, awaiting the inevitable. Then he took one step away from me, drew back the sheet, and said, "Is it all right if I touch her?"

I looked at Raya, who was standing in the door opening. She nodded.

Then the examination began.

ALL THAT TIME I had looked at her, looked at Lizzy, as my daughter. As *my* daughter. I looked at her skin, which had belonged to me; skin that was fair and intact, covered with bruises from gym lessons and a life full of fun. I looked at the hands, the broken nails where traces of paint were visible. We didn't always give her a thorough washing before she went to bed, and often made do with a washcloth: *The rest'll come off in bed.*

But her black hair gleamed as if it had been brushed that very morning.

How long does the body of a child belong to the parent? When does she lock the bathroom door for the first time, when does she hold her hands over her budding breasts, when does the sense of shame first appear—shame for her body, for the gaze of a father? When do the genes of father and daughter part, so that the young body becomes a *self*, a creature in its own right? No one had been allowed to touch her while she was alive; no one had been allowed to see her in this nakedness: this body was holy, holier than mine. She had belonged to me.

And now the doctor looked at her in my place—Lizzy had disappeared. She was a body outside of my body. Even less than that: her body was an object of study. Of horror. Of alienation.

And yet . . . in a bright flash I saw my daughter as she must have been. Perhaps for the first time I could see her without the veil of my projection: the projection of my fears and dreams, what I wanted life to be. What I wanted Lizzy's life to be. As she lay there, exposed to the eyes and the fingers of a stranger—even though it was Siebold, even though it was the family doctor who had given her her first shot, who had carefully opened the folds of her vulva, who had hung her on a hook to weigh her—under the gaze of a stranger she turned back to herself. And away from me.

This may be the only moment in the life of a human being when we show ourselves as we really are, the only moment when we are not conscious of ourselves, of another's gaze. The only moment when we don't have to prove anything to anyone: the moment when we are dead.

It was on her deathbed that I finally understood that Raya was right all along. Lizzy had never belonged to me. I had appropriated her.

(IF THERE'S SUCH A THING as a landscape of memory, is there also a landscape of comfort? Or is comfort no more than the realization that life is a series of shortcomings and inadequacies? But even in that landscape of desolation there had to be something stable, something to hold on to—a tree to hide behind, an image to disappear into, a word to take refuge in?)

THE DAY AFTER Lizzy died it began to rain. The bright blue sky that had greeted the day did not cloud over; it simply faded to a lifeless gray. In the evening the first drops started to fall, and the thrumming on the deck swelled to a monotonous murmur that continued all that night.

We kept a vigil next to her bed.

The little girl who had once been my daughter deteriorated into a ghost, a cocoon in white sheets. We sat at her bedside and observed the process of disintegration, until the body became stiff, the shadow of death passed over her limbs, the mouth tightened into the anonymous grimace of rigor mortis.

Lizzy was gone.

I drew the sheet over her face and took Raya by the hand.

We walked into the garden, where the rain had dug channels in the barren ground. It wasn't cold and the nocturnal shower was gentle and summery. Amid the rotting blossoms of the slain rhododendrons, the damp rose from the earth. Raya moved the chairs to one side, and I brought out the clean, dry bedclothes that had gone into the Miele that morning and dropped them at her feet. I went into the sunroom to get the bottle of La Mission-Haut-Brion

1991 that had been acclimating, and filled the glasses to the rim. Raya spread the sheets out over the clammy planks of the deck. We raised our glasses and drank. Then we made love, with death hot on our heels.

We drank. We cried. We made love until morning came.

"It wasn't that long ago that everyone knew where they came from, who they were going to marry, what they would become later, and how they'd be buried," Raya said.

"Very reassuring," I said and leafed morosely through the folders from Zuyderfeldt Crematory and Rising Sun Funeral Home.

The kitchen table was strewn with sober advertising material in which undertakers, crematories, "natural stone quarrymen"—who writes this stuff?—humanist counselors, and floral artists (believe it or not) extol their potential contribution to the suitably atmospheric interment of our daughter.

I began to consider placing her body on a self-constructed funeral pyre.

"Aren't we allowed to decide for ourselves?" Raya had snarled at the funeral director who represented the Mutual. We hadn't even realized that we were insured—apparently it was part of our Total Policy—and the man probably thought we'd welcome him with open arms, grateful for his advice and support. Raya was furious that he had the audacity to simply arrive on our doorstep. He must have feared that any minute she was going to grab him by the throat. It wouldn't have surprised me either.

Of course we were allowed to decide for ourselves, he hastily assured us, and he left behind the folders he'd been clutching under his arm.

"Cremation?" I said miserably.

"A handful of ashes strewn out over the sea and *whoosh*—gone," Raya said. "I can see it now."

" 'Scatterfield especially for children,' " I read aloud from the folder, " 'dotted with wildflowers, surrounded by a centuries-old hedge of copper beech. Moment of silence.' "

We looked at each other in desperation.

"Let's go," she said.

"Let's go," I said.

We packed the car and took off.

IN THE CEMETERY of a village built on a prehistoric mound, the picnic basket was opened. There was a magnificent goat cheese made with droppings—it stank to high heaven and was illegal to boot. (The Food Inspection Service says you're not allowed to use droppings in cheese, because they can make you sick.) There was a bottle of the best Châteauneuf-du-Pape I could find. And fresh young spinach leaves, tenderly layered with damp paper towels, to go with the garlic sandwiches. There was a hard sausage, a cross between chorizo and the kind with cloves that's popular in the northern provinces and that we can get only at our Turkish grocery. And there were strawberries, more than we could bear: pounds of strawberries and sugar in a Tupperware bowl.

I spread out the beach towel just beyond the shadow of the old church, between the mossy grave of Helmer Tjallens (1797) and one Tietje Wolmantel (1862). From this spot we looked out over meadows and the trained lime trees surrounding the parsonage garden. The green of the trees hung heavily from the truncated branches. The first of the leaves were already lying on the grass.

Absentmindedly, Raya picked up a few leaves from the ground. "Summer is the season when things wither and fade—fall only confirms the suspicion. And in the winter it's a fact."

We were lying on our backs, listening to the incomparable silence of the countryside: the call of a bird, water dripping into the drainage ditch, the wet tires of a car passing in the distance. We looked up when a flock of swans flew past just over our heads.

There were a few gray cygnets in the group. The displacement of air under those giant wings was faintly audible—*whoosh, whoosh.*

Then they were gone.

We walked around the old deserted cemetery. Judging by the most recent grave, the last funeral in the village had taken place in 1931. Driving in, we'd seen the new cemetery just outside, surrounded by pastureland. There was no church, only a small building for the shovels and rakes, and perhaps the obligatory cup of coffee afterward. We stopped at a small, weathered gravestone that had subsided to a slant.

AUKE, FEBRUARY 1818–MARCH 1818, the epitaph read. And underneath: AUKE, DECEMBER 1818–SEPTEMBER 1819. And underneath that: AUKJE, MAY 1820–JUNE 1823.

Raya pointed to the back of the gravestone: BLESSED THE FATE OF THIS YOUNG CHILD, SOONER IN GOD'S MERCY MILD had been chiseled into the stone.

"That takes nerve." I sighed.

"That takes courage," she said.

W E   A T E   our picnic lunch in silence. The shadow of the church shifted unnoticed across the beach towel, which was slowly becoming damp. We drank the last of the wine and fed each other strawberries and cream. Tears streamed over my cheeks and went on streaming—it was no longer crying. Raya was transparent and pale as an invalid. Her whole body trembled. I took her on my lap and drew the blanket around her. Night fell.

"I can't find the words anymore," she said, dismayed, and she gazed at the sky. "I thought . . . I thought the words would come of themselves."

After that it was quiet for a long time. From behind the parsonage the first rays of the moon fell over the churchyard. It was even quieter than during the day.

Then she slowly got up from my lap and shook off the blanket. I tilted my head back and reached out my hand, but quickly withdrew it. In the light of the rising moon I saw a once-familiar face change into the mask of a beast: her eyes widened, like marbles, the iris rolled, her mouth opened, her lips cracked until they bled. From deep in her chest I saw a scream rise; first there was nothing, a sigh, a final breath—and then across the churchyard and into the night sounded the heartrending cry of a dying she-wolf.

If there's such a thing as a landscape of memory, Raya had written, *is there also a landscape of comfort? Or is comfort simply the realization that life is a series of shortcomings and inadequacies?* But even in that landscape of desolation there has to be something stable, something to hold on to—a tree to hide behind, an image to disappear into, a word to take refuge in?

It is not time that heals wounds, but oblivion. Or—even more banal—our forgetfulness.

We tell each other tales of immortality—and that is what remains to us. That is where we live on. To exorcise our finiteness, we tell stories about how it was, how it would be. Until the stories become reality and what really was is forgotten.

TWENTY

WE BURIED LIZZY on September 5, 1996, in a small cemetery not far from the dike, where water and sky meet. There had been no new grave there for a hundred years; the nearby hamlet was long since deserted, its residents having moved to a town where there were jobs to be had at the milk co-op. But our inquiries revealed that there was no regulation prohibiting burials on this spot.

Raya sat down at the sewing machine and out of two small purple dresses she made one dress, with ribbons around the waist and long sleeves to cover the sinister marks on the arms. She dressed her, I brushed her hair. Then we laid her in the coffin, ready to leave.

Brechje and Jelle accompanied us. Together we drove north, together we carried the coffin, together we lowered her into the grave, together we covered her with rich clay soil. And on her grave we planted a young star apple.

We found rooms next to the café in the nearby village and drank until dawn. Then we went back to the grave. It was covered in flowers, notes, stuffed animals, drawings, and balloons.

The obituary card had reached those who had loved her in time.

JELLE SOLD LITTLE HEAVEN to a project developer before a single nail had gone into the wall. He and Birgit moved into a penthouse not far from where we lived. Brechje left for the States at the invitation of MIT, where she had been offered a fellowship. Her star rose quickly in the world of theoretical physics. She married a blind pianist and was a faithful correspondent.

ON MY BIRTHDAY, two months after Lizzy's death, Raya gave me a volume of poems. She had compiled it herself, and had it typeset and bound in leather. "It's as good a place as any to start all over," she said. We traveled in the footsteps of the poets.

When we returned to Holland we went to see Lizzy at the foot of the dike. The flowers had wilted, the paint on the drawings had washed away, the slab was buried under rotting leaves. We gathered up the litter and cleared the grave, to give the little star apple more room.

Someone had planted a cutting next to the grave. It turned out to be a rhododendron.

3

Do

TWENTY-ONE

PROPHECIES HAVE DISAPPEARED, tongues have ceased, knowledge has been destroyed. All we have left is a tender young fossil eating its way into the most recent layers of our memory. That childish face has become fixed, her image forever imprinted, never again visible other than in the afterimage that gleams in the morass of our memory.

And beneath that morass her life rocks gently in the old bog, halted at five years: after 60 months, 160 weeks, 1,820 days, 43,000 hours of life.

THOUGHT HAD LOST all vigor. At first, thought had served as a fig leaf for our shame. We were ashamed of the ancient stigma of parental dereliction: we had been unable to spare our child an early death. We were ashamed of the pathos attached to the death of a child, the pitying looks to which there is no answer. You feel guilty when you are at fault; shame is what you feel when you are the victim.

We were ashamed of still being alive.

We countered shame with reason. She did not die in vain, we said to each other: she had been a muse. She had given us infinite love. She had bound us to one another forever: more than our marriage, more than her life, her death—one and indivisible—belonged to both of us. The wedge which parenthood had driven between us had been bridged—no, it was not a bridge: grief was more like an enormous boulder that had become detached and had rolled down the mountainside, blocking off the chasm and linking our mountaintops to one another.

But grief is not a boulder. You can't kick it. You can't smash it to bits by sheer willpower. You can't get around it or over it. Grief happens to you. It paralyzes you. The grief of her death was a dense mist that descended on us, sometimes stealthily, sometimes with treacherous rapidity; it blocked our view and yet gave us nothing to cling to. We had hoped to bridge the divide, to cross over, but that was a fata morgana. The boulder turned out to be a white cloud.

WE HAD NO VOCABULARY to describe where we were standing. Mourning is so all-encompassing that words become trite: melancholy, sorrowful, somber, depressed, sad—the words were there, but they lacked precision. That Eskimos need multiple words to describe the snow they see around them every day was something I understood all too well: when we speak of life and death, words cannot be precise enough, or the underlying meaning subtle enough. Under arctic conditions, it is important to know the nature of snow—the cause, the incidental circumstances, the location, the quantity, the density—and the consequences. All this must be captured in that one word; otherwise the word itself is useless and doomed to extinction.

The danger inherent in the existence of words is that you use them, for want of something better; you use them to clarify something, but they only cloud the issue. The danger of shared grief is that you think you are sharing it, you think that the words you exchange and the tears you shed are comprehensible to the other person. That is at least as dangerous as using the wrong word for snow.

The ice hole lurks: ah, you understand.

(No, I didn't understand. But that's water under the bridge. After one of us has fallen into the ice hole.)

T H E   R O A D we were on led nowhere.

N O T   O N L Y   W A S it chillingly quiet in the house, now that the childish voice had been silenced, it was also quiet inside us, between us. "Words were not made to be lived in," Raya said, and she exchanged the notebooks for her laptop. She filled all those extra hours with writing. I took shelter in the darkroom and bent over the poems. "You can go on aestheticizing until you're blue in the face," she'd said, "you'll still be none the wiser. It'll still be your way of filling in the emptiness." That's where I now found myself. The emptiness refused to be filled; the emptiness could only be made bearable by approaching it from a different angle. I studied the poems and looked for the metaphor.

When winter came and the first hesitant snowflakes fell onto the cold ground, I couldn't stand it any longer. My heart turned to ice. The decision was quickly made. We sublet the house through a reputable agency; Raya packed the suitcases, stored our personal belongings in the attic, and closed her laptop in preparation for our departure. We hadn't set a date for our return. We would stay away until spring—and it was up to us when spring arrived. We took off on a sunny winter morning, in the direction of the German island of Sylt.

I   N E V E R   R E A L L Y   B E L I E V E D that there was a landscape of memory; I never believed in the landscape of comfort. Raya's sentences fascinated me, touched me, but they remained an abstraction. Her ideas formed a rational construction that she decked out with words, like silver ornaments in the Christmas tree: beads and mirrors for the soul. But there on the beach, on

Sylt, a tiny ray of light broke through a blanket of clouds. It wasn't tangible; it wasn't yet an insight. But a vague suspicion was growing that behind the blinding force of words there was a truth, and that the truth she was trying to put into words was bigger than the words themselves.

> *The next tide wipes across the mudflat's path,*
> *and everything on all sides grows alike;*
> *but the little island out there has closed*
> *its eyes: the dike circles confusingly*
> *around its dwellers, who have been born*
> *into a sleep where they get many worlds*
> *mixed up, silently: for they seldom talk,*
> *and each sentence is like an epitaph.*

THE ISLAND WAS DESERTED, and if there was any life there, it was enacted behind closed shutters and curtains. It was the day before Christmas, and even the fishing boats remained in the harbor. Night fell at four o'clock in the afternoon.

We found rooms in a weathered *Gasthaus* on the beach; it was closed for the season, but the owner was willing to open one of the rooms for us, albeit unheated. We were given a hot-water bottle to take to bed. The *Familienzimmer* on the ground floor featured two breakfast tables, eight straight-backed chairs, and a large tiled stove, on which we sat huddled together, drinking *glühwein* until our cheeks were as warm and red as our buttocks. We took long walks and went to bed early. Now it was Raya who slept, Raya who every morning crept farther into the depths of the enormous eiderdown, with no sign that she would ever get up again. As weightless as I had felt when our daughter was staying overnight with friends, that's how ponderously Raya seemed to fall back to earth now that she was gone. More irresistible than gravity was the attraction of the bed; it weighed her down, hid her away.

In the early morning I tiptoed out of the bedroom, drank the landlady's coffee, unmistakably diluted with chicory, took a bite of the sweet white bread, and headed for the beach. Over the water there hovered an unreal gray morning light that was not caused by fog or by clouds. It was as if the sun had lost some of its vigor and was shining over the island at half its normal strength. As a precaution I was dressed like an arctic explorer, but the winter cold was also halved, tempered by the surrounding seawater, which was now warmer than the land.

Along the dry flood line, a life was on display: rope and nets, bits of tar and dead fish, the skeleton of a bird, a shoe, a wooden crate. It was a life I couldn't relate to, a life that belonged to fishermen, beachcombers, and outdoorsmen. I had to settle for the role of observer.

SINCE THAT LAST DAY of August I hadn't been able to sleep; nothing helped, not even the eiderdown and the hot-water bottle. Fatigue made me reel, the bitter taste of coffee and chicory burned in my mouth, and I was so light in the head that it made me dizzy. But I kept on walking. There was no reason to go back: I knew I wouldn't be able to sleep. Numbed, I planted my boots in the sand and fixed my gaze on the expanse of wet beach in front of me, resolving to go on walking until I dropped. But again and again I was halted by all those objects from another world that imprinted themselves upon my retina. As if the whole beach were strewn with them. I tried to think, but the only thoughts that came were: Fish. Shoe. Rope. Tar. I tried not to think, to just follow the path set out by my feet, but that didn't work either. My brain foundered upon the unbearable realization that there was nothing more to understand. All that was left was fish, shoe, rope, tar. *And everything on all sides grows alike.*

(I REMEMBER back when she was learning to talk. I remember especially clearly the time before she could talk. Every chair leg, every zipper, every shoelace, every *thing* was deserving of her undivided attention. Each object at her eye level was worth examining—not silently, not patiently, but noisily, and with the intention of understanding it as quickly as possible by taking it apart. Before she could walk she knew how to dismantle the remote control. Before she was toilet-trained, she had discovered how the record player worked. To her, the hinge on a kitchen cabinet was as profoundly interesting as the leather-bound spine of a literary masterpiece.

And as she carried out her investigations, she talked: in an endless stream of gibberish, she provided a running commentary on her explorations, issued orders to herself or to the innards of the alarm clock, and aimed magical incantations at the gears on my bike. The fact that no one understood her was of minor importance. What mattered was that the object she happened to be concentrating on at that particular moment understood her. And the objects did understand her. At any rate, she felt understood.

When, according to the statistics of the child-care clinic, she was too old to go on babbling away in her own language, we launched the offensive: armed with the classic picture books, we taught her the meaning of words. We taught her that the wind doesn't listen if you give it a talking-to, that pebbles don't answer when you ask them a question. We taught her the difference between I and You and the rest of the world. We taught her to communicate.

The result was that the stream of words dried up and she took refuge in paint and brush. As fanatically as she had dissected the world, she painted what was left, but the laugh was gone. And I saw on her face the first signs of humanity, the veil of loneliness. The world in which she had been one with objects crumbled, dwindled into short words, sloppy sentences, questions that were urgent but unintelligible to us. The inability to express herself, the impossibility of knowing that she was understood, seeped inexorably into that childish head. Words silenced her. The fall from paradise had begun.)

MAYBE IT WAS the chronic lack of sleep which manipulated my consciousness; maybe it was due to the unreal light, the stillness of the beach, the absence of a horizon; maybe it was some kind of mental short-circuit caused by months of aimless grief.... Maybe it was something I shouldn't even be talking about: the fact that my mother appeared to me there on the beach.

She didn't materialize out of a hazy cloud, she didn't arise out of the gray waves, she didn't descend from the heavens—no, she quietly caught up with me from behind and put her arm around my shoulder.

I recognized the pressure of the hand that rested on my forearm. "What on earth are you doing here?" I said.

"There's no road back, my boy. You'll have to keep going."

"What road, Mom? What are you talking about?"

"Once you've started off, all you can do is to keep going. Your destination is fixed."

"What a ridiculous idea!" I said disdainfully. "Everything is wide open. What's more: everything is wide open all over again."

"Love rejoices with the truth. It bears with all things, believes all things, hopes all things, endures all things. But it does search for the truth."

"It doesn't endure all things. Love has its limitations too. No one knows that better than you."

"Just as you're looking for love, it's looking for truth, Gideon. There is no answer to your questions."

"Is that your conclusion," I suddenly heard myself shouting, "after sixty-four years of life? Is that the truth that's supposed to make me *rejoice*? That there isn't any answer? Is that why you came, to tell me that?"

Now she was silent.

"Words are seldom the beginning of insight and much too often the end," she said finally.

And each sentence is like an epitaph.

"And you?" I said softly. "Where are you going?"

"I'm here. With you."

"Is that your destination? With me?"

"More than anywhere else, my boy."

"That's definite?"

"That's definite."

She pressed the Mamiya into my arms. "There's no road back, my boy. You'll have to keep going," she repeated herself. "Look! Look around you, Gideon."

"But where do I start?" I asked. "Where should I start, Mom?"

The arm around my shoulder fell away. "It's already begun"— her voice sounded from ahead of me—"It's already begun, my boy."

I STOOD on the flood line holding the Mamiya, which seemed heavier than ever. I looked around me. I stopped thinking; I *saw*. I saw images all around me, strewn at my feet like the remains of an airplane after the crash. The emptiness in my head filled up with the objects on the beach, filled up with the surge of water that was slowly rising to just in front of my feet. The tide was coming in.

Near a weathered tangle of nets I squatted down. Like a hunter aiming his gun, I brought the camera to my eye, patiently waiting until the rising tide appeared in the viewfinder and was just about to wash over the net—and then I pressed the button.

TWENTY-TWO

"WHAT DO YOU THINK about when we make love?" I asked.

"I don't think."

"Well, what do you do?"

Raya was silent.

Later she said, "Why do you want to know, anyway?"

"It's something I've wanted to ask you for years."

"Since when?"

"Since the first time."

She was looking at me and smiling.

"Well?"

"Well what?"

"Well, why didn't you ever ask?"

I was silent, listening to the murmur of the sea that carried for miles across the valley and up to the balcony of our *casa rural.* The sky over our heads was black as ink and strewn with galaxies whose existence I had never suspected. Behind us, where the Spanish village ended, the mountains loomed, tall and black as the sky. From open doors and windows came the sound of conversation, sometimes snatches of song, often drowned out by agitated television voices. Children were playing in the conduit running down the middle of the street.

WE HAD SET OFF from the far north in the direction of spring—which here began in February. We had originally planned to travel on from Sylt to St. Petersburg, but after checking the weather, we changed our minds. It was below zero there.

The trip was nonstop: drive four hours, sleep four hours. After traveling for two solid days, we arrived at our destination: a village on top of a hill, at the foot of the mountain range, with a view of the sea. The air was lukewarm. Here spring began three months early.

We arrived early in the morning, together with the fishermen who were just hauling their wooden boats up onto the beach: these were the drifters, the pirates, who—weather permitting—spent all night at sea and then sold their illegal catch in the marketplace or to the smaller restaurants. Before the sun had reached the mountaintops, we were already sitting next to them in a café, eating silver-colored fish that curled on the grill and bone-dry fino. It was six o'clock in the morning, and after less than forty-eight hours, Sylt was a season away.

When the sun reached its full strength, we took refuge behind the massive walls of the old house where we'd rented a room. We slept the day away and didn't wake until dusk had fallen and a large flock of sheep was noisily wending its way through the narrow streets of the village. The chorizo and the cool manzanilla next to the bed tasted good; naked under the sheets, we tentatively reached out to each other. In the shelter of the early dusk I walked over her body with my fingers, touching each and every freckle and birthmark along the way; the tight little wrinkle under her navel, where her belly had been so taut that it had torn beneath the skin; the scar between her shoulder blades; the small callused hands. And from there further, and further, into the unfathomable depths. As the outside noises died away unnoticed and the sky darkened, we lit a candle and struggled to find a way back to ourselves.

WHAT WAS I THINKING about when I made love to her? The absurdity of the question became clear to me in the restatement. We hadn't made love in years, at least not like before, not like those first nights in her icy bedroom-on-the-beach. Is it possible to make love to a pregnant woman? There are men who claim there's something erotic about it, and some women become terribly sexy during pregnancy. It has nothing to do with love: it's the hormones taking them for a ride. I once saw a whore in the red-light district who was a good seven months pregnant. The men were standing in line.

Is it possible to make love to a mother? You're not welcome and you know it. But you pretend, and she pretends. You know she'll never say, "Gosh, I'm sorry, but I'm sort of busy at the moment. Caring for your progeny. You've become irrelevant." Sex after conception is a fact after the fact. The ultimate superfluity. But just try bringing up the subject. We had never been able to.

It's often occurred to me (although I've never dared to say so out loud) that it is dangerous to allow a man anywhere near the bedside of a new mother. It's the equivalent of libido assassination. Other cultures are better at such things: the man has no business being there; it's women's work. Let them hold one another's hand; let them bring on the damp cloths and peer between one another's legs. We men should be spared such things: the moment when the magic of a woman is transformed into an enormous reproductive machine—the once so voluptuous flower ripped open like a rotten pomegranate, the once so alluring scent mingling with blood and excrement, the beckoning lips sliced open like the flaps of a cardboard box—my God! In that instant the potency of the male of the species flies out the window. He has served his purpose. He is free to go. While she—that desirable body of hers—has become an instrument. Ready to give birth, to nurse, to slave, to keep watch. Ready for the next litter.

No, the arid loins of the barren woman are more seductive than the warm loins of a mother.

What did I think about when I was making love to her? I worshipped her like a goddess because her body had carried our child. I despised her because of the rejection which it brought me. I wanted to make love to her as a woman, but the child always came between us, and stayed between us. I wanted to merge with her, but I knew that my place had already been taken.

I hated that magnificent body.

> *Through the street without a person*
> *a black horse passes by,*
> *a wandering horse*
> *a horse of evil dreams.*

(And Raya slept on, as if tomorrow didn't matter. The night was cool, the heavy woolen blanket followed the contours of her body. Through the open window the light from the streetlamp fell on the tiled floor and the white-plastered walls. The room was a tabernacle in which she lay enshrined like a precious jewel. I picked up the sketchbook and stared at the woman I had to learn to love again. The sheet remained blank.)

> *The breeze from the west*
> *blows in the distance,*
> *a window might be complaining*
> *with the wind.*

THE CAFÉ in the Plaza Major opened at the first ray of sunlight. I drank my coffee and read the poem by Federico García Lorca with my sketchbook on my lap. The shepherd trudged past with his flock; a boy was hosing down a pigsty. Women were standing in line for bread; men were having their first glass of beer. I sketched a black horse; a pack mule served as a model.

Whether the village is in Holland or the far south of Spain, mothers everywhere are old for their age, I observed morosely. Old, slovenly, and washed out. The varicose veins, the heavy thighs, the frumpish dress, the unshaved armpits...the practical short hairdos recall a head once crowned with luxuriant jet-black curls, and the melancholy faces suggest that a vibrant young woman full of promise once inhabited the passionless body. The laughter and chatter of the women waiting in line to buy bread had the same ambiguous quality as in the recreation room of an old people's home: it wasn't interesting, but it served to pass the time.

As if for these women, too, life had already been given away.

There must be a conspiracy between a woman and her body, I mused: an unconscious, obsolete anticonception mechanism continues to function, even though it is no longer necessary. As soon as she has gotten herself married off and her sexuality is no longer a promise but a threat, the hatch is closed and locked. After the first, or maybe the second child, the butterfly changes into a hairy caterpillar, designed to keep the men at bay. It is a form of protection that we see all over the animal kingdom: the more unsightly, the less chance of being devoured. They make themselves invisible, the mothers, in the hope that they will be unapproachable.

Is there no longer any passion in them? Do these tired bodies, behind the facade of past glory, feel no longing, no hunger for gratification? Or is their fear of the consequences—the fear of being overrun by their own offspring—greater than their desire?

The greatest rival of a husband is not the milkman or the window cleaner, but the showerhead and the electric toothbrush. But even that was hard to visualize, looking at those Spanish women standing in line.

AND THEN I saw Raya heading down the steep path in my direction. I wasn't expecting her; it was still early. I could tell that she didn't expect to find me there either. She thought she was unseen. It's at moments like this that the other person is most visible:

when we look through the plate-glass window at the unsuspecting object of our gaze. She was wearing a long black dress and a heavy woolen cardigan, her dark hair in a bun at the nape of her neck. She shielded her eyes with one hand, the morning light was glaring. She seemed to blend in with the background, her Spanish blood just under the skin. And yet she didn't fit in—not here either. She remained a passerby in her own life.

Crimson lips. Olive skin in the shadows. How beautiful you are, I thought. How can you be so beautiful? How dare you be so damned beautiful. *You . . . mother.*

"Want to go home and make love?" I grinned when she saw me sitting at the table.

She ignored my suggestion and ordered a *carajillo.*

"I want to take pictures of you," I said, after I followed her example and ordered a brandy with my breakfast.

"What kind of pictures?" she asked. "Portraits? Pornography? Art? What did you have in mind?"

"You," I said evasively. I had no idea what I had in mind.

"By the way . . ." Raya said with a searching look, "what do you think about when we make love?"

"I FEEL LIKE going for a walk," I heard Raya say.

"Hmm."

"The barman said there's a path leading up to that little hamlet. There's supposed to be an inn there, run by Germans. Or Danes."

I had my nose in an English-language newspaper. It was a couple of weeks old and I'd found it lying behind the pinball machine in the corner of the café. *USA Today*—I had no idea how it had gotten there. Maybe left behind by those Germans, or Danes. Reading old news always gave me a carefree feeling; old news is less alarming than new news. Especially if it's American.

The sunlight had now taken possession of the entire square, but it wasn't burning hot. We were on our third brandy. My sense of time and place slowly faded. The old newspaper justified my inertia: life would go on in any case.

"How about it?"

"How about what?" I said distractedly.

"Don't be so vague," she said testily. "Shall we go for a walk?"

"I'm okay right here."

"So am I. But I'd like to see some people. Besides villagers," she added.

"Germans," I said.

"Or Danes."

It's a known fact that your orientation toward the world becomes blurred when you surround yourself with villagers, especially when you don't understand their language. It's like reading out-of-date newspapers: deceptively reassuring. But at that moment there was nothing I wanted more than to be deceived. Reassuringly deceived.

"Better call first, to make sure they're home," I suggested, with barely concealed reluctance. The mountain slope behind which the footpath disappeared looked quite far away and steep.

Raya called. The Germans (or Danes) turned out to be a Dutch couple, Sjef and Sonja, affable forty-somethings with a guest house but without ambition. Sonja offered to come and pick us up in the car: they weren't that far away as the crow flies, but with all those hills and dales... I began to suspect they were hungry for company, and I was right: when we arrived, the table on the patio was set for four and the rosé was in the cooler. Sjef greeted me with a hug. That made my day.

ACTUALLY, we were already more than a little drunk. Actually, I didn't think much of Sjef and Sonja. Actually, I wanted nothing so much as to explore the possibilities of our sagging bed with Raya. Actually, I didn't feel at all comfortable with the whole situation.

But deep down there was also a sense of relief: relief that for a short time we wouldn't be thrown back upon ourselves, that we could break out of the vicious circle of silence and understanding. The danger inherent in every marriage is that the dynamic becomes a goal in itself rather than a means; the danger of a marriage-under-threat is that each partner recognizes the other in the repetition of moves, and that both are hoping for a tie. We'd left each other in peace for too long.

But that's the kind of thing you don't see until later.

To make conversation, I started telling them about an article I'd read that morning in my *USA Today*. A mother named Susan Smith or Susan Jones—a name so common that it sounded like a pseudonym—had strapped her two small sons into the back of her car, driven into a lake, and then opened the window and made her way to the surface. The boys, obviously, had drowned.

Then she gave herself up to the police.

What I had read was not in fact a firsthand account, since the World News page had been torn out of the newspaper. But the letters-to-the-editor were full to overflowing with moral indignation, not to mention appeals for the return of the death penalty in the state where it happened. The Beast had reared its ugly head, was the general drift of the vox populi. "Especially the letters from mothers," I recounted. "They were absolutely brimming with tears and murderous intent."

"That's all projection," Raya muttered, as she expertly speared another fried sardine from the plate.

"Projection of what?" Sonja asked, unsuspectingly.

I had gathered that the couple had no children: the number of cat's tails that brushed my legs was significant. Sjef lovingly tossed the bones over his shoulder.

"Yeah, how do you mean that?" I joined in. "Are the tears projection, or the thirst for blood?" Imperturbably, Raya bit into the narrow back of a sardine. My question rolled off her back.

Sonja pulled a wilted leaf from the bouquet on the table. "I don't have any children," she said after some hesitation, "but I don't believe that killing your own children springs from evil."

"Are you going to tell us that it springs from goodness?" Sjef asked profoundly, as he pulled at his eyebrows. I considered saying something nasty about his quasi-intellectual pose, but the rosé had put me in a conciliatory mood.

Raya ignored both of them. "Do you remember the words of Medea, at the moment when she realizes that she is going to kill her sons?" she asked me. "When the nursemaid says, 'Do not give up hope, madam, you are not leaving here for good,' and she says, 'Ah! I will see others leave first. O! abomination!'"

"Schizophrenia. Is that it?" Sonja said, as if she had just been granted a valuable insight. "I once read something about women who hear voices and then go out and do terrible things. And they think it's terrible too, you know, when they hurt themselves or others. I mean, it's not as if they're happy about it or anything."

Raya shot her a venomous look. I knew that her fury wasn't directed at Sonja personally, but the poor woman cringed.

"There's a physics experiment"—Raya continued to hold forth—"in which two hemispheres are placed together and a vacuum is created in the space in between them. You can ask yourself two things. Is each of the two hemispheres an entity in itself, or do they only form an entity when there is a vacuum between them? Does the vacuum give meaning to the hemisphere? If good and evil pull hard enough at one another, the result may be a moral vacuum. But you could also reason that if polar interests that belong to each other, may even be meant for each other—attract each other, what happens then? They're riveted to each other, but outside of that, there's nothing there! Emptiness! A vacuum!" She looked around the table, visibly pleased with herself.

And then I turned vicious. It was the heat, it was the rosé, it was the brandy which had been doing its work since early morning... but most of all it was my Raya. Her self-important crimson lips were like a red rag to a bull.

"But now, Raya," I said, "do you suppose you could just tell us what you think? Or shall I get you a pen and paper so you can write a little note—you can pin it to the paella, perfect!—so the others have a fighting chance of following your brilliant reflections?"

"Medea's motive," she said coolly, "was revenge. Revenge was the reason she killed her children. But underneath that veneer of primitive rage—which I guess most of us could somehow understand, if we really tried—there's the hint of a much more existential fear. Or rather, there's the danger of an existential loss. The loss of her dignity. When a woman is in danger of losing her dignity, Gideon, she is capable of anything. That goes beyond good and evil. It even goes beyond the question of guilt."

"Aha! The dignity of the woman will always triumph! That's what you always keep in reserve: the extra supplies in the pantry, the small change in the sugar bowl, the emergency exit. This morning I looked at the women at the bakery and I was surprised by their collective ugliness. But it isn't ugliness: it's the true nature of women. You seduce a man for his genes, his money, his status—but in the end it's that so-called dignity of yours that prevents you from truly giving yourselves."

"You can only bet on one horse, Gideon."

"And which one might that be?"

"Have you ever noticed how a man thinks and talks about parenthood? His emotions aren't rooted in his fatherhood, let alone his thinking. For a father, it's always a kind of moonlighting. He looks at his newborn baby the way a scientist looks at a new invention, proud of his experiment. With a remote kind of interest, he bends over the petri dish in which a speck of cloned mouse is floating on the surface."

"Well, it does happen to be his own clone."

"Don't talk nonsense. The man is a father as long as the child is there. As soon as it disappears from his field of vision—the father disappears, too. He's just a man again. And a woman is supposed to cast her lot in with someone like that?"

"So that's the unreliable horse you're afraid to bet on?"

"It's not just that. Dedicating yourself—that's something you do only once in your life. A one-off. Never again. Just think back to the conversation with your mother on the beach on Sylt: a meaningful encounter isn't necessarily an event between two people. And you don't always need two for conflict, or alienation. All those processes of becoming one and separating can also take place within one individual, one mind, one soul, one brain. Whether the other is a man or a child, the hemisphere of a woman is stronger than the vacuum she creates with either of them."

In the meantime the cats had extended their domain and were now walking unhindered across the table, searching for remains of the lunch. Embarrassed, Sonja and Sjef continued to look straight ahead, one still plucking at the centerpiece, the other at a cat's ear. By that time I was so beside myself (because of the alcohol, because of Raya) that I didn't give a damn. Besides, they didn't have any children. So what did it matter?

"Well," Sonja said, "how about if I drive you two home?"

"Are you crazy?" Sjef said jovially. "Nobody's driving anybody anywhere. We've all had too much to drink. Do you want to stay overnight?"

I looked at Raya. Raya looked at me.

"We'll walk," she said.

"From here it's downhill all the way." I grinned.

TWENTY-THREE

In Italy she said, "It's a story about love, and it's finished."

She closed her laptop and went back to pen and paper.

During those last weeks in Spain she'd typed as if possessed. The explosion at Sjef and Sonja's had had a chastening effect on both of us—the poisoned apple had been dislodged from Snow White's throat—and we were able to get back to work. The fear of going on living gradually gave way to relief that there was a life worth living. Raya bought an electric kettle and a jar of instant coffee, and in the half light of early morning she sat at a table by the window with her laptop. I lay in bed and looked at my wife. I took photographs: not pornography, not art, but a multiple portrait of what was most dear to me in this life. I'd gotten the first tentative sketches for Quasimodo down on paper. "This is about love, too, you know," I said, and showed her my sketchbook.

She leafed through it thoughtfully. "You draw well," she said after a while. "Where would you be without hands?"

"A photographer without sketches," I said. "How about you?"

"A writer. With two feet and a head."

Later I asked, "What would you be with your hands tied?"

"That's perverse." She smiled. But no answer was forthcoming.

WE TRAVELED over the Pyrenees for that one poem, even though I could just as well have taken the pictures in Spain. But where that's concerned, I'm a puritan: I never try to put anything over on people. I have this conviction that you don't have to be an expert to see whether a photo is authentic or not—a somewhat outmoded principle, now that every Tom, Dick, and Harry has a digital camera and can touch up any imperfections in his creation with the help of his Apple. But I'm a child of the Moro reflex. I have to feel what I see to know for sure. I have to see what I feel to believe that I am safe.

Raya understood that: for her part, she was glad to see her fountain pen again, even though it continued to leak uncontrollably. And I was glad to see her again: a mop of hair bent over a pile of yellowed notebooks that she'd found at the local grocery; grouching about the wobbly table on the edge of the sidewalk, with a glass of wine in one hand and the leaky pen in the other. I secretly took a couple of pictures from the balcony.

The question had not yet presented itself, but I knew that it was in the air: what now? Her legitimacy had disappeared; the reason for her peaceful coexistence lay far away, deep in the clay of Groningen. Raya was literally left empty-handed. And the more passionately she scribbled in her notebooks, the more certain I was that this question was also on her mind. But when do you suddenly look up and say, What happens now?

When does that indefinite "now" become imminent? When I thought about the child's weathered grave, about the hardwood floor and the black streaks made by the shoes of strangers, I felt a mixture of dread and homesickness. I wanted to go home, and I feared what was waiting for me there.

THE JOURNEY HOME presented itself, but that was not of our doing. It was late afternoon—I'd spent the whole day in the mountains, roaming around in search of just the right light to capture the last verse: *the flower that whitens the olive groves in among jonquils and blue of flax.* I was on my way home from the mountains and from far off I saw Raya sitting. She looked up and waved.

"It's a letter," she called, "from Brechje!"

I put my photocase down on the bench leaning against the warm wall of the guest house, went inside to get a wineglass, came back to where Raya was sitting, and allowed the news to sink in. A letter from Brech. Here in Italy. What did it mean?

"How?"

"General delivery," Raya said.

"Yes, but how? How did you know that there was a letter for us? How does Brech know where we are? The whole thing is crazy!"

Raya looked up in surprise. "What's the matter with you? Why are you getting all upset over a letter?"

"I'm here for my work, Raya. I've spent the whole day tramping the mountains. I got some really good shots. I'm already thinking about a new series. Damn it all, I've got other things on my mind than the life and work of Brechje Kalma."

"What's your problem?"

I couldn't describe it, but it was as if the world were suddenly closing in on me. As if life were closing in on me. As if the question of "What happens now?" had suddenly pounced on me—and was now pressing me for an answer.

"Never mind," I said in a growl, and I picked up the envelope from the table. It had been sent to the Oude Houtstraat with a request to forward it—there was nothing strange about that. The agency always had our current address. The people who'd sublet our house had forwarded the letter to the agency; the agency had seen that it got to the local post office here in the village; the landlady had been given the mail when she went to the shop. Raya was right: what was the problem?

"What does it say?"

"Read it."

"Not now."

I put my arms behind my head and closed my eyes. The slanting afternoon sun bathed my face; a slight breeze blew up through the narrow streets of the village. For a moment it was quiet. I thought I could hear the distant chirp of crickets which had accompanied me all that day in the hills. The olive trees appeared on my retina, the young shoots in the arid hillside fields, the blue sky dotted with tiny white clouds, high up and far away. If only I could pare away the months that lay behind us, the months that lay ahead of us, like the rind on a piece of cheese. It was good, the way it was now.

"SHE'S PREGNANT," I heard Raya say.

"Good for her," I said, and I kept my eyes closed.

But when I opened them again a little later, she was gone.

IT WAS LATE in the evening when she got back to the guest house. I'd polished off the bottle of wine she'd left on the deck. After that I fell asleep in our room. Hunger woke me; it was late in the evening. Downstairs in the café I ordered bread and a plate of spaghetti. Absently I leafed through a copy of *Gazetta dello Sport*, and sat watching a nude quiz show on TV. Halfway through my second glass of wine I saw her come in. Without saying anything, she sat down next to me and poured herself some wine.

"Where've you been?" I asked, and I stroked her windswept face.

She didn't answer. I handed her the bread, and she dipped a piece in my plate and ate it.

"Did you read the letter?"

I shook my head.

"They've had an amniocentesis done. They know for sure that the baby will be blind."

"Because of her?"

"Because of him."

"It must be a relief for her," I said in all honesty. Now Raya was silent as well.

We walked outside, away from the light. It was so dark out that we could barely see each other. In the shelter of the night, Raya became calmer; I heard her breathing slow down.

"You asked me where I was," she said, "but even if I told you, you still wouldn't know. The night's so dark, maybe I don't even know myself. Sometimes it's hard to recognize where you are or where you've been. The surroundings can interfere with your orientation—or the time of day or the way the light falls or the thoughts in your head. And suddenly you think: where on earth am I?

"I was down by the harbor; the smell of fish is still in my nostrils. There was a low-hanging mist; the water cools off faster than the land.

"I think about Brechje," she continued. At this moment she has a child; in a little while it'll be gone. Her eyes are failing; Carl's already completely blind. It's too much for her. At this moment she has a child, in a little while it'll be gone—and it's her doing. For a short time—a month or two, maybe three—she was a mother, and then never again. That's it. Her decision."

The wind blew up; it turned cold around us. The night was moonless; the darkness enclosed us. Chills ran down my spine, but not because of Brechje, or because of her child. I'd heard the story, but I wasn't listening. I didn't want to listen. I wanted to be as deaf as she was blind. I didn't want to hear any more.

"Hush," I said softly, and I took her hand. But Raya wasn't listening.

" 'Just one day,' she wrote, 'I was a mother: just one day, there was trust. After that came the doubt, then the test, then the doubt, then the decision. Just one day a mother, just one day the commitment that it demands. And now it's gone.' But was she a mother? Did she *become* a mother? Or is that status reserved for women with a full-term baby? When are you allowed to call yourself a mother, what are the decisive criteria: conception, pregnancy, full term, the delivery, the nursing, the care? How many ordeals must you endure to be worthy of the prize? No one will ever call her Mother. No one will ever blame her for her flawed motherhood—so flawed that the child did not survive. And she will never be able to share with other mothers her motherhood, that fleeting moment, that fraction of time when she discovered that she was more than one. I don't feel sorry for her. She made a choice, and there's no need to pity anyone because of a choice, even when its effect is disastrous. But I wonder, I can't help wondering..."

"...whether you're a mother or not."

"What it is I am now. You can't mother when there's nothing to mother. And yet...you were once. You were a mother. You've been one, you were one, and yet you don't know what it is."

"Like a writer without hands."

"Like a writer without a story."

WE LAY IN BED and neither of us could sleep. We were on the same track. The darkness made me brave: "Why did you run away?"

She said, "Go to hell," and turned her back on me. After that it was silent between us, and the church clock chimed away the hours of the night. It was not a moment for love.

"When are we going home?" I asked, after hearing the clock strike four. I imagined that I saw light through the window. The back moved slightly, but did not turn.

"I'm ready to go."

"What are you going to do when we get back?"

I felt how she turned toward me; I could have seen her face, but I remained on my back and looked at the ceiling.

"What are you going to do?" she asked.

"Akhmatova," I said.

"Then I'll go with you."

IT WAS TIME TO GO. Spring was coming; it was getting warmer in the south. What remained was home—and St. Petersburg.

TWENTY-FOUR

SHE SAID, "I don't want to become anyone's memory," but after she left, the house was full of her: her image, her words, her thoughts. I was overwhelmed by the emptiness: I reached out to an image, but it turned out to be her hologram; I thought a thought, but the words turned out to be hers. I looked at my house and it was her space. I tumbled, first slowly, then faster and faster, into emptiness, in free fall not so much through lack of a handhold as through lack of substance.

The air resistance was zero.

THE MADNESS tore through my brain, leaving devastation in its wake. Like a hurricane, it raged through the remains of my life: the components were arbitrarily erased, ravaged, sucked up, and then deposited elsewhere, fragmented and unrecognizable. I cleared a path through the battleground of my memory, clutching at any object that seemed faintly familiar, but it turned to dust in my hands as soon as I picked it up.

Stability proved to be dissolution. Shelter a ruin. The oasis a deluge.

I CLEARED OUT the house as a means of repossessing the territory. The nursery that was once a junk room (and had been returned to that state)—out. Our bedroom with the wrought-iron three-quarter bed that we'd had made to our design—out. The garden, overrun by every kind of greenery known to man—out. The deck, rotten to the foundations and hollowed out on the spot where her chair had stood—out. And finally the living room: 350 square feet of indestructible inner-harbor teak, cut to size, sanded and varnished—out. I stripped the house down to the frame, and what remained was a pile of bricks.

I was left with a megalithic tomb.

IN THE MIDST OF THE CHAOS, one image survived: the breakfast tray she'd carried into the bedroom on our daughter's birthday, the day of Raya's disappearance. Covered with a damask napkin, a small lighted candle in a candlestick. Toast done in the oven, tart marmalade. Poached eggs. Six roses in a small vase. The wind toyed with the white curtains. The coffee was hot and strong.

Two old, tender hands placed the tray on my lap.

Her kiss, wet with tears.

> *Night came on and in the dark blue sky,*
> *Where the Jerusalem church so recently*
> *Shone with mysterious splendor,*
> *There were only two stars above the tangle of branches,*
> *And snow flew from somewhere, not from above,*
> *But as if it rose up from the ground,*
> *Indolent, cautious and tender.*
> *That day my excursion seemed strange to me.*
> *When I went out, I was blinded*
> *By a transparent gleam on things and faces,*
> *As if everywhere lay petals*
> *Of those pinkish-yellow, smallish roses,*
> *Whose name I can't recall.*
> *The windless, dry, freezing air*

So held and cherished every sound
That it seemed there was no such thing as silence.
And children were shoving their mittens
Through the bridge's rusty iron railings
To feed the greedy, gaudy ducks
That somersaulted into ink-dark circles in the ice.
And I thought: it's not possible
That I will ever forget this.
And if a difficult path lies ahead for me,
Here's an easy task for me—
Be it in old age, in sickness,
Perhaps in abject poverty—to remember
This raging sunset, and the exuberance
Of spiritual strength, and the charm of sweet life.

TWENTY-FIVE

Jᴇʟʟᴇ ᴅᴇᴄɪᴅᴇᴅ to move in with me temporarily, after finding the entire contents of my house at curbside, awaiting the garbagemen. The time had come to intervene. I was not receiving treatment, and I was not suicidal: with the checklist on his lap, Dr. Siebold had ascertained these two facts, following a series of intensive sessions. The medication was adjusted; the social network closed around me. But I wasn't crazy.

A letter came from Brechje in which she urged me to come over and spend Easter with her and Carl—a check was enclosed, together with a flight schedule. The letter remained unanswered. My brother Herman who, except for his one-night stands, was pretty much at loose ends, came by every week with a bottle to get drunk with me. Birgit signed me up for the latest service provided by her business empire, an upscale variation on Meals on Wheels for the discriminating yuppie: every night it was grilled lamb chops, bisque of scallops, or Caesar salad with a multigrain loaf topped with sunflower seeds—delivered to the door in a box, complete with linen napkin and a friendly smile. A girl from some unimportant magazine I'd once worked for arrived on the doorstep (her name was Jorien and she'd been in therapy herself, so she knew what I was going through and wanted to be there for me). She made a very unstable impression, but for a nominal sum she cleaned the house once a week. I suspected her of masochism. And finally, a moving van pulled up in front of the house, with the compliments of Mrs. Ripperda. Since the tragic death of her husband (said the accompanying letter), she was thinking about moving into something smaller. My "emergency" was an excellent opportunity for her to carry out an initial selection. In my stripped-down living room her designer light fixtures resembled intestinal polyps, and the mechanism of the state-of-the-art Auping bed was far beyond my technical insights, but what did it matter? I had light in the living room and the mattress was soft.

DESPITE THE STATE of mental havoc in which I found myself, my business affairs were flourishing—entirely unknown to me. Jelle had examined my photos for the poets series and then secretly sent them to a distinguished British magazine, where he knew someone on the editorial board. *Global Village* replied by return mail with an advance of 3,500 pounds.

Jelle took my hand and led me into the darkroom; together we bent over the negatives and contact prints. (The reason for all this sudden activity escaped me, and I suspected that he and Siebold had cooked up some kind of occupational therapy for me. For the past few months I'd spent most of my time lying on the couch with reading matter of questionable quality.) We examined the images with a magnifying glass, and discussed focus and lighting. After that I withdrew and got sloshed on his mother's lime-green chaise longue.

Efficiently, Jelle saw to it that the photos were printed as agreed during our discussions, and then sent a set of prints to London. The money poured into my bank account, and still I knew nothing.

THERE CAME A MOMENT—unexpected but inevitable— when I walked into the kitchen to find Henk Siebold and Jelle Ripperda seated fraternally on either side of the table, their hands restless, their faces worried. In front of them on the empty table lay the small volume of poems Raya had given me; Jelle's hands were folded around it as if it were a relic. He fussed nervously with the clasp. "There's something I have to tell you," he said. (The preamble was superfluous: his whole lanky body was in penitential mode, as if he were anticipating a serious talk with his mother—I'd seen it many times.) And then he told me about the volume of poetry he'd found; the negatives from Spain, Italy, Sylt; our discussions in the darkroom; the prints he'd had made. About the response from *Global Village*, and the series that had created a furor in the magazine and far beyond.

About the money that was pouring in.

The talent that was being wasted.

I sat there in the kitchen, unshaven, amid the smoldering ruins of my life (or my past—that distinction had not yet been made), at his mother's exclusive Moldani table, with a fourteen-carat hangover and a mug of black coffee.

Four piercing eyes, directed not at the tabletop, but at me.

Siebold began: up to now the medication had done its work; the psychosis was under control. But there had been no further progress; he feared a standstill (and a standstill meant decline, he hoped I realized that—it was something I could just grasp). He knew a psychiatrist, actually a friend of his, retired. Excellent record of service. Trained as a neurologist. They'd discussed my case: interesting, artistic, promising. It might just be an idea, in view of the lack of progress....

And in walked, deus ex machina, J. C. Bilbrig—neurologist— and shook my hand with great conviction.

(JUST BEFORE you drown there is a moment of choice. This has been established by research based on the testimony of drowning persons: those who had survived a shipwreck, but also those who had come to the assistance of others shortly before they actually drowned. It had always been assumed that death by drowning, aside from the physical condition of the victim, was related to the person's expectations in this life. In other words, it was assumed that, percentage-wise, those who were wealthy, happily married, well-adjusted, and hardworking had a better chance of surviving than those who were already perched on the brink of disaster.

But the reverse was true.

Those who fought against death, who were in a state of mortal fear, were the first to go under. Those who fought for life, whose only concern was saving their own skin, were the ones who made it.

Fear of death is nothing but fear of life. And sooner or later fear proves fatal.

That was what was going through my mind as I looked into the pearl-gray eyes of J. C. Bilbrig—knight in shining armor.)

THIS WAS THE PLAN: while awaiting the results of the investigation into Raya's disappearance, Jelle and I would complete the poets series, starting with Anna Akhmatova. The real mourning could not begin until there was certainty about what had happened to her, and that certainty might be long in coming. Nevertheless, it was important to start reliving the past, in order to take leave of it (Bilbrig). The circumstances in which this would take place would be surrounded by every conceivable safeguard (Siebold). *Global Village* was financing the trip to St. Petersburg for the two of us (Jelle).

Stunned speechless, I listened to the trio: Huey, Dewey, and Louie had their roles down pat. Jelle put the tickets on the table; Bilbrig took out his organizer to set up dates for the support sessions; Siebold showed me the prescriptions for the first-aid kit, should anything untoward occur along the way.

I felt the water rising to my lips, ready to swallow me up.

INSIGHT USUALLY follows choice, but once in a while the two coincide. That morning at my kitchen table—which wasn't my kitchen table—I acted without thinking, thought without feeling.

I no longer felt anything: I let go of the life raft and plunged to the bottom.

THE WATER closed over me. On the surface a small circle appeared, and another and another, until a constellation of circles was floating over my head. Tiny fireflies danced before my eyes, specks of light: gray and blue. I looked up and saw a white sky, in which the black ice hole was mirrored like a giant cloud in negative.

For a fraction of a second I had grasped the truth, as transparent as the light on the beach on Sylt: she could never have meant for me to give up my life. I had to read her poems; I had to learn to read her again. There was no need to go to St. Petersburg. I myself was the ice hole in the Neva.

I FINISHED my coffee and nodded to the gentlemen. I took the volume of poems from the table and closed the kitchen door behind me.

A YEAR HAD GONE BY, twelve months in which life had beaten the living daylights out of me. I'd taken what was meted out to me; I knew all about the weak spot in my defense.

I left the kitchen, went up to the landing, and took hold of the string hanging from the attic to pull down the ladder. I mounted fifteen wooden steps before my head was level with the floor. The attic had been straightened up; the smell of cooking oil and roll-your-own tobacco was gone. Dust danced in the light. In the corner, in the dusk, lay her old trunk. I knelt down and undid the two straps holding the lid and the trunk together. The lock opened with a click. The contents of the trunk were covered with a linen cloth. Carefully I removed the cloth and laid it on the wooden floor.

On top lay a photo of Lizzy, an ordinary snapshot of a grinning child with a mop of black hair and green eyes. She was wearing a white dress and she was barefoot. I saw the bruises on her knees, the grime on her face. I laid the photo to one side.

There lay Raya's life: the photograph album, letters, notes that I had thrown out and that she, apparently, had retrieved. Notebooks with scribblings, short stories.

One by one I picked up the papers, looked at them, and laid them to one side, layer by layer, patiently, carefully, in the conviction that there was a vein of gold gleaming in the depths.

And there was: it was a pile of papers, held together by a hemp rope.

With great care, I replaced the contents of the trunk and closed the straps. I took Raya's volume of poems, the photo of Lizzy, and the pile of papers, and lay down in the light of the tiny attic window, with my head on the linen cloth.

I cried until it was soaked with my tears.

Then I undid the knot in the string and began to read.

TWENTY-SIX

Dear Gideon,

If there has ever been a moment in my life when I was happy, it was the moment that I genuinely believed I was: the moment when time converged and past and future touched, when I gained insight into the meaning of our existence, when my own life was as insignificant as it was indispensable.

(The way she lay there on my belly, a butterfly in her cocoon; having entered the world with a scream that sounded from both our throats, crying over the life she had not asked for, but I had nonetheless given her. There was no going back, and we both knew it. I suspended my disbelief and decided to love her.)

How much happiness can a human being endure?

Happiness is nothing but the sincere conviction that you deserve it. It only happens to you maybe once in your life, which is probably a good thing.

I loved her, Gideon, more than anything in the world.

But man does not live by love alone.

My mother loved me, too, but she made impotence into an art form. Renouncing life—I fear that mothers are past masters at it. They do it with the best of intentions: in order to pilot their child safely into the

world. But beneath the patina of that glorious destination, decline
reigns supreme. My mother knew it, and she always blamed me. I, in
turn, always felt I had a right to blame her for that—but now I know
better. Who could possibly be the cause of her ruin except me?

You can't go on reinventing your past. How many times must you
rewrite the story before you can say, Now it's finished? It is never
finished, never complete, never good enough. So you have to make
the decision to end it. That's the way it is. That's the way it was. This
is my story. It has nothing to do with truth: you make your past into a
tolerable lie. It is only when an event becomes a memory that it is
harmless. It is no longer something that happened to you; you have
appropriated it. It becomes a story you can pass on. A story others
can build on.

Motherhood is life's greatest lie. It is an illusion that must be kept
alive at all cost, because it encompasses our own existence: the
existence of mankind. It is where truth and untruth are so close to one
another that there is no space between them.

Why is a child born in pain? To spare the mother. The pain of
childbirth dulls the other, more fundamental pain of the loss of
yourself. After the birth of Lizzy I screamed it out: why didn't anyone
ever tell me how excruciating it is to bear a child? But that's not
true—they did tell me. I was prepared. And nevertheless I was
overwhelmed. That's the way it has to be: the pain of childbirth
cannot be imagined.

And that is why we forget. We forget that we pass through the
gates of hell in order to give our child the gift of light. We lose the
memory, because somewhere along the way we have lost ourselves.
In every childbed, a life is placed in the offertory box.

We know it, and yet we pass it on: life. The precious lie of
motherhood.

I know of no important woman artists with children, a well-known
woman writer once said (she herself is still living with her mother,
even though she is well into her forties—the ultimate paradox). Of

course she doesn't know any; there are no important women artists with children. How could there be?

The essence of creating is that the entire creation originates in your own brain, that you are lord and master of it, genesis and end result. That one day you are able to say, This is what it was meant to be; it is finished. You can do it with marble or clay, with your personal history, even with your life. But not with someone else's life.

Let alone the life of your child.

That restriction is built into the creation of a child. It is as elusive as water: one moment you think it's there, but before you know it, it's gone. For a woman artist it is an intolerable thought that she will never be the only creator, that she will never see the end result of her creation. Of course she can say, This is the way you should be; now you are finished—but the child goes its own way and leads its own life. It does not allow itself to be nailed to a pedestal.

(But how do you make use of the emotion you feel when you look at the face of your sleeping daughter? The cliché lurks, ready to pounce on your mother's heart, ready to snatch the words from your pen. The focus slips through your fingers. I am afraid to summon concentration for fear that it will be disturbed again: child and writer are in a permanent state of war—a war to the death.)

There are no important women artists with children; the two quantities cannot coexist. Motherhood is fatal to imagination. Imagination is fatal to the child.

The day that Lizzy was born I made a decision: I was prepared to do anything to unlock the secret. I wanted to know exactly what it was like to be a mother, what it meant to be a mother. It was something no one had been able to tell me, not even my own mother. Lizzy was going to tell me. Together with her, I would make *motherhood* into a work of art, a creation that would grow under my hands.

She was not the object; she was the material of my creation. She was the clay in my hands, through which I would give form to that unknown, unutterable something that transforms a woman into a mother.

But what happened: I came to love her, more than anything in my life. I came to love her during the nights when I nursed her, when I took her temperature, when I chased the crocodile out from behind the curtains; when I calmed her fears—helped her to come to terms with life.

Under my hands love grew, a love that would never again let go of me. Motherhood proved a cruel pursuit—and I loved her.

Set off against that one heroic moment of giving birth, there are the countless senseless acts which are necessary to perpetuate her life, necessary to ensure that you do not come to grief yourself. But the meaning of life cannot be survival. At least, not under ordinary circumstances.

From her birth my existence had been relinquished; I had strung the beads of time together, but earned no necklace in return. How is it possible that a woman allows her hours, her days, her entire life to be wantonly obliterated? The chronic fatigue of the mother is not the result of the lack of sleep: it is the result of the lack of sovereignty.

You are no longer the master of your own life—and everyone considers this normal.

There wasn't one moment of the day that I wasn't on call; not one moment of the day that she wasn't in my hands, in my heart, in my head. I thought, One day this will be over; one day she will be older and I can begin to sweep together the shards of who I was. But that moment never came, Gideon, and I realized that it would never come.

A mother will never again be sovereign, never again autonomous.

What replaces all that is a dedication, a selflessness that transcends humanity. Perhaps that is the work of art they call motherhood: the sublimation of the concept of love.

All these insights came together on board the *Schöne Erna*—or to be precise, just before then. Over the years, I had recorded everything pertaining to my life with Lizzy: trivial observations, great thoughts, the words she learned, the incidents that had made us laugh or cry. Four years of my life, meticulously recorded and documented, as if it were the logbook of Columbus—but writing a logbook doesn't allow you to experience the voyage; recording the coordinates doesn't mean that you have reached your destination.

I went away in the hope of finding myself, not as a mother, but as a human being. I wanted to know what was left of me. I was in pursuit of my imagination.

And then she called me back. The message came that she had fallen through the ice, that her life was in danger. She had called me back!—not as a human being, but as a mother. In the hospital I looked at my daughter, near death, and I knew: for all my talents, I was helpless in the face of such violence. There is no defense against one's love for a child.

How can I tell you what happened after that?

I came back and I told Lizzy all the stories that I wanted to share with her. I burned the notebooks in the garden, and then I buried the ashes. In the early morning of her fifth birthday I went into her room. It was dark outside, and warm. I lay down next to her in bed and I looked at her: this being, this gift that had hollowed me out from the inside so that she herself could grow. I felt such infinite love for her. I took her in my arms and rocked her; half-asleep, she opened her green eyes, and I said, "I love you, Lizzy." Then we fell asleep. At the first rays of the sun, I awoke. I must have cried; the pillow was soaked. I took it out of the pillowcase and lay down on my daughter. I gave her a long kiss, and then I pressed the pillow over her sleeping face. Briefly, there was resistance, but I pressed the full weight of my body on that small body that had been born out of me—and then it was still.

She would be with me forever.

In the months that followed, together at one remove from our life, I found the words to describe what it means to be a mother. Even now, I do not fully understand, but I do know that it is only in the imagination that lies and truths can be merged into one and the same story.

This is my story, the book I had to write—as a mother, it would have been impossible.

What happens after this, I don't know. It may be possible to get over the death of a child, but you never recover from the love for a child.

Not until all my words have been used up can I reach the emptiness.

Just as a lie drives a wedge between lovers, the truth will do the same. This is my truth, Gideon, and it cannot be shared with you. If I had shared it, you would have left me. If I had lied to you, alienation would have been the result. Now, at least, I have kept my promise: to be a memory together. To be a single story.

I am sharing with you the only truth that I have, in the hope that I may always be known as: wife of Gideon, mother of Lizzy.

Raya Mira Salomon

Epilogue

THIS WAS THE STORY of Raya Mira Salomon: mother of Lizzy, storyteller, liar. My lover for seven years. She left me a trunk full of papers, the reflection of her life. The image that rose out of this legacy was as intangible as she herself had been all those years. She reached out to my longing for something to hold on to, although I knew that it could never be satisfied: I would never know who she was, at most who she had been.

After her disappearance I wanted to forget as quickly as possible, but the book that she left me made that impossible: sharing this truth with her demanded my unconditional surrender. I accepted the challenge.

The presumption of death, for which I submitted a request to the district attorney, was granted two years later. It was the only way of keeping her in my life, of holding on to what the three of us were.

Even now I don't know whether everything that is written here actually happened that way. It doesn't matter anymore. It is the truth; it is a truth: it is a story.

I will say no more.

I give you my wife, Raya Mira Salomon.

ACKNOWLEDGMENTS

Grateful acknowledgment is made to the following for permission to reprint material:

Jack Bevan: Excerpts from "Homecomings," from *Quasimodo: Selected Poems*, translated by Jack Bevan. Penguin Books: U.K., 1965.

Zephyr Press: "Epic Motifs," from *The Complete Poems of Anna Akhmatova*, translated by Judith Hemschemeyer, edited by Roberta Reeder. Copyright © 1989, 1992 by Judith Hemschemeyer. Reprinted by permission of Zephyr Press.

Rutger Kopland: "Like playing with water itself, playing with the thought . . . ," English translation by David McKay. Courtesy of Rutger Kopland: *Thanks to the Things*. Copyright © 1989 by G. A. van Oorschot Publishers, Amsterdam, The Netherlands.

Farrar, Straus & Giroux, LLC: Excerpts from "The Island" from *New Poems* by Rainer Maria Rilke, translated by Edward Snow, published by North Point Press. Copyright © 1984 by Edward Snow. Reprinted by permission of Farrar, Straus & Giroux, LLC.

Mercedes Casanovas Agencia Literaria: Excerpts from the Spanish poem "Las cinco. Potro," by Federico García Lorca. Copyright © Herederos de Federico García Lorca. Translation by Barbara Fasting.

The story of the blind photographer is based on the article "Een mens ziet wat hij weet" ("One sees what one knows") by Reinjan Mulder, inspired by an exhibition of the work of the blind photographer Evgen Bavcar (*NRC Handelsblad*, November 13, 1992).

The passage on memory that opens chapter six was inspired by the introduction by Wim Kayzer to the book *Vertrouwd en o zo vreemd—over geheugen en bewustzijn* (Contact, Amsterdam, 1995).

The quotation "I don't know of any important female artists who have children" is taken from an interview with Austrian writer Elfriede Jelinek and Anneriek de Jong (*NRC Handelsblad*, September 25, 1998).

ABOUT THE AUTHOR

Maya Rasker studied German linguistics and literature at the University of Utrecht. *Unknown Destination*, her first novel, was long-listed for the Netherlands's most prestigious literary award, the Golden Owl 2001, as well as for the ECI Book Award. She received the Golden Dog-Ear Award 2001 for best literary debut of the year. She currently lives in the Netherlands with her two daughters.